# A Fine Piece of Chocolate

*Righteous Sistas Crossing Over to the Wild Side*

JACQUELINE R. BANKS

WestBow
PRESS
A DIVISION OF THOMAS NELSON

WestBow Press books may be ordered through booksellers or by contacting:

WestBow Press
A Division of Thomas Nelson
1663 Liberty Drive
Bloomington, IN 47403
www.westbowpress.com
1-(866) 928-1240

ISBN: 978-1-4497-9109-4 (sc)

Library of Congress Control Number: 2013906390

Printed in the United States of America.

WestBow Press rev. date: 05/07/2013

There comes a time when one has to take stock of their life circumstances and ask, "how did I arrive here?" It was an initial rush, being away at college. Ohio State University, with its diverse student body and campus activity, was a far cry from the Sumpter Houses of Newark, New Jersey. Although Gloria and Kim had a mom-daughter relationship that many would envy, based upon genuine respect and camaraderie, nothing, but nothing could compare with living away from home.

It is so important to choose one's friend's wisely. Living in close quarters with an individual who's upbringing and life choices are the polar opposite of the values that you were born with presents a challenge, particularly if the sheltered individual did not have to make contrasting choices while they were in the sheltered environment. Let us examine Arneatha's character.

Arneatha is a friendly young woman who can pull others to her like a magnet. Growing up in an environment where she saw too much too soon and learned that adults, particularly the ones responsible for her safety were not to be trusted, led her to develop a rebellious, self reliant streak. In her words, "my mom and dad, they weren't really mom and dad in the traditional sense. They were cut ups. Mom was crazy and had to be hospitalized twice. Dad tried to play dad when he was home. I'm not sure if all my sisters and brothers at home were dad's kids. My mom went out with Willie, the number runner, who gave her food money when the month was too long for the money. Willie couldn't be trusted, though; he tried reaching for my breasts one time when I was eleven and I smacked him and ran away. I think he was shocked that I had such nerve at such a young age."

Kim (watching Arneatha smoking a cigarette across from her in the dorm room), "Arnie; aren't you scared the matron will smell that cigarette and put you on probation?"

"What?? Are you serious? Kim, I got big time issues you know nothing of. Following rules? Which rules? Who makes the rules? Oops, I forgot. Church girl! Gotta follow the rules. (mocking tone)

Kim shriveled inside at the hurtful tirade. While believing in the righteous way, she didn't want to be ostracized and singled out negatively by somebody so worldly wise. Quickly, Kim shifted the topic to the upcoming African American Student Union dance. "Anyway, what do you think you'll be wearing? Girl, I know you'll be styling and profiling. Arneatha, (smiling, mood swiftly changing). "Yeah, you know that's right. Think you'll be going?"

Kim—"I'm not sure, but yeah, I might go."

Arneatha—"Don't you usually meet with that Fisherman's Club on Friday nights?"

Kim—"Oh, you mean the Fisher of Men Club. Yeah, we meet about twice a month. I think I might check out the AASU dance.

Arneatha—"Yeah, go ahead, I know the sisters can break loose in the spirit. My aunt took me and my sisters to Southern Baptist every now and then. Nobody could move like a sister in the Holy Ghost.

(Fast forward to the night of the dance).

Several of Arneatha's friends stopped by the dorm at 6PM for an early dinner of General Tso's chicken and lo mein. Kim feigned a smile at their loudness and boisterous discussions of their encounters with their boyfriends, and what women they had to put in place. While she thought she could cram some last minute studying for the philosophy midterm on comparative religions, that thought was quickly scrapped over the din of noise from the raucous laughter.

Smoke from the curling iron filled the room, along with the cigarettes that Arneatha and Lavonne kept smoking. While not a smoker herself, Kim offered a couple of saucers for use as ashtrays. "After all, (Kim reasoned to herself) why not make friends of friends comfortable?" The girls continued to exchange gossip on who was hooking up on campus, who thought they were cool with their man but was really getting played. Kim wondered to herself, when ever did they have time to study, but then the focus shifted to Arneatha's wardrobe. The girls oohed and aahed when Arneatha pulled out the black monochromatic leggings set by DKNY. The knockoff Tacori gem necklace provided a striking contrast against Arneatha's mahogany colored skin, along with the floral I.N.C. dress.

Meanwhile, Kim pulled from her wardrobe the Donna Karan jeans and ruffled blouse with a slight cleavage, along with the knee high boots that Gloria gave her last winter (a safe choice) she thought to herself. Arneatha, after studying Kim's choice of outfit stated, "Kim, that's OK, but I have something that can really hook you up. "But", Kim protested, "this is cool." Arneatha suggested something cooler still. (Ignoring Kim's protest), "Lavonne, get that dress, you and Kim are the same size." Lavonne quickly obliged and went back to her dorm room, returning 30 minutes with a spaghetti strap floral print above the knee. "Now, try this one on girl. Trust me, I know how to hook you up." (Turning to Bridgette), "Bridgette, you're the curling iron queen, hook her up now. (To Kim) "Trust me, I know how to hook a sista up."

Kim sat in mute amazement as Bridgette parted her hair, zigzag style, and then worked her magic with the curling wax and the curling iron. Upon changing into the spaghetti strap mini, and seeing her new 'do in the mirror after Bridgette was done styling her hair, Kim jumped up and down and screeched, "wow! Thanks a million Bridgette," and gave her a big hug. "Kim," (said Arneatha) show what you got! Nothing wrong with that, right? Go ahead church girl. Ha ha I'm only playing."

"Absolutely stunning!" Kim thought to herself, amazed at the transformation. It was a bit more skin than what Gloria would have approved of. College becomes a place where, on your own, choices are so numerous and opportunity beckons like a finger. Being a young adult with a strong academic mind and upbringing offers some protection. However college is still a place where peer pressure can and does rule. Choices build one on top of the other until they bring a person to their present place.

(Setting at the dance)

At the dance, young people from all over the African diaspora collected in the common space called Blaine Hall, sporting locks, perms, warrior haircuts. "What up, Kim?" Tyriek high fived her. He was the friendlier of the twin brothers in Kim's biology class. Soon, Kim became aware of a slight, pungent odor in the room. "Weed", she thought. (**Evil communication corrupts good manners**), a verse from Proverbs that Gloria often quoted to Kim. Nevertheless, Kim got swept up in the atmosphere of music. The DJ played a combination of old school R&B, today's R&B and gangsta rap. He was a talented master mixer. Becoming aware of the glances from some of the young men on the dance floor as Kim danced to her own beat, she observed all the fashion statements, from haute couture to near naked. Welcome to the 21$^{st}$ century.

Soon, the DJ played a set of slow jams. Kim stood at the outer edge of the dance floor, watching couples slowly grinding as Aretha crooned, "Ain't no way for me to love you. Slim, with his bulging biceps and Stacy Adams shoes asked, in his baritone voice, "may I have this dance?" similar to the way guys asked girls to dance when Gloria was coming up, Kim thought.

Slim held her close until she could feel his bulging manhood. (Gloria's voice: don't be easy. Put value on yourself and don't follow the crowd). Kim wanted to pull away from him, but instead, rested in him and let him hold her.

Kim's first year in college is an experience in choices. College, especially when living away from home, is an experience that cannot be repeated again. The choices made there, however, stay with us in our minds, and in our bodies. There is no mom and dad to confide in, but, if one looks hard enough, there is that guardian angel; that mentor, or that voice from within.

**(For the good that I would I do not: Now if I do that I would not, it is no more I that do it, but sin that dwelleth in me.) Romans 7:19 &20**

*Chocolateism: Maintain your integrity even in the atmosphere of compromise, for it only takes one step in compromise, to start losing character.*

# The Dilemma

Why do righteous women hook up with unrighteous men who cause nothing but drama and pain? It may be because people are not one dimensional. We all have our public face that we must present to be found acceptable to society in order to get rewarded: that income; stay in the good graces of the family circle or that sisterhood of friends and coworkers. Then, there is the me that nobody knows and, let's face it: isn't it easier to confess that you're having a hard time paying the bills than a hard time keeping your legs crossed? Women will get silenced for that transgression quicker than, let's say, gossip, which can actually kill someone's reputation. The ladies represented in this story are struggling to keep their passions in check until the right man comes along and puts a "ring on it."

*Remember your values from home*

I have a special fondness for Kim. Kim is at a vulnerable age, at the crossroads of womanhood. Although raised in Newark in the Sumpter Houses, Kim was blessed to have been born to two parents married to each other, who loved each other "till death did them part." Paul and Gloria Smith were part of a visible, but fast disappearing family structure in the inner city; the nuclear family.

Paul was a family man who had a strong work ethic from his native Barbadian upbringing. He was a quiet man whose presence was nevertheless felt both in the home and in the surrounding community. Young boys out in the community, "proving themselves," would stand tall and say, "hey Mr. Smith" and let him pass by before continuing with their foolishness. Paul had a special fondness for his firstborn, Zodie, a learning disabled child who was a bit more immature than most youngsters her age. Paul said on more than one occasion, "I'm a law abiding man, but I tell 'ya, let some rascal touch me daughter, and I will blast them away, ya here?"

"O honey, you musn't say things like that. Nothing's gonna happen to Zodie, I'll take care of her."

"Sweets, you don't see things out here the way I see them. These people you know, they will smile in your face and hurt you in a minute."

Kim smiled at the memories of her mom and dad's conversations that she would overhear sometimes. Paul had a particular love for the "three ladies in his life, as he called them, and he had a unique ritual for each of them. He would read to Zodie her favorite book and chapter that interested her, on his days off. He would share with Kim the stories about his native boyhood in Barbados and explain the fine nuances of fashion. He once surprised Kim with a manicuring kit from Bloomingdale's and explained to her the difference between looking polished and refined, vs. looking fast for the moment. "That's like the race horse who bolts the stall first, but finishes last." As a pre-teen, Kim didn't always understand and fully pay attention to her dad's words, but now she wishes she did.

## Make your boundary lines clear, or someone else will draw them for you

Kim had to admit, with guilt mixed with pleasure, that the Saturday night dance at Blaine Hall was stepping over the boundaries somewhat. The dress she wore that she borrowed from Lavonne did, in what would have been in Gloria's words, covering next to nothing, and then . . . being in Slim's arms for the slow jam. Being in Slim's arms literally caused Kim to inadvertently gasp and felt a pleasurable rush in the center of her being, with his manhood up against her womanhood. When she tried to pull away from him a little bit, he held her closer.

"Kim! Kim! Wake up!" Arneatha's rough voice snapped Kim from her daydream revelry. "Girl, you've been like, zoned out." (Curiously) "Somebody got your nose open?" "No, nothing like that" Kim responded to Arneatha's probing. "Look, you could tell your big Sis," Arneatha said teasingly." Well," Kim started slowly, not sure if she shoud confide her feelings to Arneatha. "Do you know anything about any of those guys at the function?" Arneatha responded, "what, you stupid? You know how many dudes been at that function? Who do you mean?" Kim (by now getting used to Arneatha's sharp tongue and wit) trying to sound as casual as possible, "oh like Memphis."

Arneatha—"you mean, Slim. I know he used to be with this older broad, Julie. She has her own place. I think she hooked him up with clothes and money, I guess he was a kept man. (pausing) . . . you're not into Slim, are you?"

Kim "No, not at all. He's just so good on the dance floor.

Arneatha—"nah. I don't think you would be in his league, not yet anyway.

Kim is already becoming sexually curious. The emotions and fantasies that Kim secretly indulged in, to push out the reality, that actions have consequences: **Sow a thought, reap an action. Sow an action, reap a habit. Sow a habit, reap a destiny.**

Being on the cusp of womanhood and making life challenging decisions has led many a righteous sista off of the straight and narrow. Already, Kim is starting to daydream more, study less, and her grades are starting to slip . . .

"A C minus?" Kim blinked her eyes several times, holding the test paper. "Oh, who cares about Plato' and Aristotle's theories about life? This too shall pass." Mei Wing, who was part of the group project that Kim participated in, looked up from her desk, startled at Kim's attitude. "Ah, Kimmy, you don't mean that, no?" "Well, whatever," Kim snapped. Mei Wing winced, a bit startled. "What's with you, Kim? I thought you liked this class." "Not this one," Kim responded. Mei Wing tried again to reach her friend, "maybe I see you at the Fisher of Men Club Friday?"

Kim continued walking away, and Mei Wing wasn't sure if Kim heard her or not.

The boundary lines are shifting: you become like the company you keep. As one's interests begin to shift, one loses track of the old values, which, if not reinforced, grow dim over time. It's now been three weeks since Kim has attended the Friday Fisher of Men's Club. Several members of the Fisher of Men's club ran into Kim in the school cafeteria. "Hi sister Kim, praise the Lord. We haven't seen you lately. What happened?" Patty asked with genuine concern. Kim gulped and responded, "uhm, I've been falling down with some of my grades this semester and I have to devote a lot more time to studying." "Okay, Kim, we'll be praying for you, OK? The Lord will help you study more and pass all of your classes."

"Thanks", Kim smiled weakly. (thinking to herself), "Well, it is true, I do have to study more and bring that C- to a C+ or even a B-.

Righteous values grow weaker and weaker, the longer you stay away from them. The pull of natural desire and distractions grow stronger and stronger. Kim felt a pang of guilt at having lied to her Christian friends about studying. To ease the guilt, Kim took out the large, Introduction to Psychology textbook. "For an introductory book, it sure is heavy," Kim thought. How much intro does one need?"

Having the time alone to herself, with no distractions, gave Kim ample time to study Sigmund Freud's theories on human behavior. The bottom line, everything boiled down to one's sexual desires. Freudian theory, which once seemed boring, grabbed Kim's attention.

*Distractions: A Detour to Success*

The rustling of silverware caught Kim's attention as she was answering the last fill in question at the end of the chapter.

"Mind if I sit here"? the young man in the blue plaid shirt and dress trousers motioned to the empty table and chair next to Kim. "No", Kim feigned a smile. She really wanted to reread the chapter one more time so that the info could stick in her brain. The young man taking her smile as an invitation, proceeded to continue talking. He held out his hand, "my name is Eric". Kim took his hand, "Kim." ("Well", Kim thought to herself, he seems to have nice manners. Most guys don't extend their hands to shake in an introduction.") "So, what are you studying?" Eric asked.

"Oh, Psych 1, PSY 101, sect. 10, Kim answered.

"I mean, what is your major?" "Oh, social work or media. I really haven't decided yet. I was just rereading____Eric cut her off in midsentence. "The Black Student Union is hosting a benefit for Haiti. I was wondering if you would want to contribute?

"Oh", (Kim felt somewhat disappointed at the query) "Well, I can't give something now, but let me read that brochure in your hand and I will get back to you," Kim promised.

Eric expounded upon the evils of U.S. imperialism and how we have to help our people throughout the African diaspora. Kim closed the textbook and listened to Eric expound upon Afrocentric theory and how the Europeans did not understand our culture and forced their Eurocentric views upon "first peoples" and we have been living in last place ever since.

Kim and Eric exchanged cellphone and email addresses, and over a period of time, began a friendly exchange of discussions on values. Kim maintained that while values can change due to the circumstances one finds themselves in, there really are a set of core values people must live by. Eric maintained that values are not fixed, and each person must decide for him or herself, what to believe in, especially when the dominant culture forced values upon us that were not ours. At times, Kim found Eric rather irritating and a diversion from her studying as she struggled to bring up her "C" average.

# Caution:
## Dangerous Crossing

Kim is getting more and more drawn into the social aspect of the college experience. Signs, if you will, are put out there for us to draw back into the safety zone. The familiar postcard from Newark, New Jersey came to Kim's mailbox. Kim felt a pang of guilt as she remembered how she started to answer her mom's last letter and thank her for the package, but set it aside. Kim ripped open the envelope and began reading: "Dearest daughter: I was thinking about you this week. So much is happening out here. It looks like the City is going to raze a shopping mall around here, and they may use eminent domain to force out some of the existing businesses. Oh boy! Just like the Devil or the world: they offer you something with one hand and take away with the other. Did you receive the package? I didn't hear from you. I hope you are keeping up with your studies and keeping in the Way. I love you, you know. I know Zodie can't go to college; she would if she could. Remember the child of God I know you are.

Kim quickly closed the letter as a lump in her throat suddenly came from nowhere. "Mama, you know how to hit where it hurts", Kim thought. "I'm gonna write you this weekend, I promises" Kim decided to call Eric, as listening to him, even if she didn't understand the point he was trying to make at times, was interesting nevertheless.

"So, maybe I could bring some of the CDs by my group, the Soul-A-Dad trio, to your crib", Eric suggested. Kim suggested, as an alternate, listening with their earphones in the library or in the lounge. "Ok, but you can't bring food into the library, and I thought I'd treat you to some General Tso's chicken."

At 7PM, Friday, Eric came by Kim's dorm room. Arneatha was out with Bridgette and the rest of the crew. Eric carefully laid out the napkins, plasticware and Styrofoam plates. He dished out the General Tso's chicken and yellow rice. He used the plastic ware even with the chicken pieces, and was careful not to drop any pieces on the comforter.

"Everything about him is so meticulous and well thought out," Kim thought. She instinctively moved closer to him. Kim listened politely to the Soul-A-Dad trios CD. It really wasn't her type of music, with the heavy metal sound fused with rap and R &B. "How do you like it?" Eric asked. "It's nice. It takes some getting used to." Kim felt her eyelids get heavy and she began nodding, as it was near her bedtime. "It's past someone's bedtime," Eric said teasingly. He put his middle and index finger under Kim's chin and moved in to kiss her. Kim instinctively backed away and laughed. "Guess it's time for you to leave then." Eric took her by the hand and lifted her to her feet. He walked to the apartment door, and as he turned to leave, he stopped and studied Kim's face up close for a minute. "I like you, Kim. I really do." Kim felt her heart begin to pound in her ears as Eric leaned over and kissed her. He teased her open mouth with the tip of his tongue. "Oh my goodness, this feels so-o-good, too good to be true" Kim thought as she placed both hands around the back of his head. "Be my girl?" Eric asked. (I'll think about it,") Kim thought. Instead, she sighed a breathless yes. Eric kissed her again before he left, closing the door behind him. Kim felt the familiar throbbing sensation in the center of her being, but this time it was even more intense than when she was slow dancing with Memphis Slim. "Wow! I got a boyfriend now. I know I got to be careful."

Kim now is starting to enter into the danger zone. She is dealing now with sexually powerful feelings towards someone who is not walking the same path that she started on. From their conversations, he believes in acting on impulse because, in his words, "we are adults, after all, and we determine our own values. You don't need anyone to guide you." Kim, on the other hand, was raised with two loving parents who guided her in the righteous way, and the importance of saving herself for someone who will provide for her and take care of her, the way her Dad to her mom. (*The unmarried woman careth for the things of the Lord, that she may be holy both in body and in spirit . . . Romans 7:34*)

A boyfriend is not a substitute for a husband, and many a young woman feels such an attachment to the young man she is with, that she cannot see a future without him. Kim and Eric had many philosophical discussions, but the humanistic point of view of self determination and make your own values is the antithesis of the views Kim's parents schooled her in. Emotions just don't stand still. They lead one somewhere.

There is something in human nature where people are often attracted to opposites: someone who is different from us. Differences bring about excitement. With differences comes a need for conflict resolution, and for the intellectual mind, this is a reason for being, and for a college girl crossing over into womanhood, decisions will be made which will last a lifetime. Drama makes the heart beat fast. Sometimes, danger can look like love. Can sistas find real love with a man whose values will eventually cause friction and pain? Is friction and pain secretly attractive? Kim will have to answer that one for herself by the end of the story.

# Is the Cup Half Empty or Half Full?

What are you saying, O Lord, to the Kim's of today? Kim is a representative of today's Generation Y: tech savvy, multi-tasking experts, megabytes of info that comes at them in a quantum leap, entrepreneurial and can turn to a new job as fast as one can flip a burger. But still, these are young people and they are vulnerable. The age old questions of how far can I go, and yes, no. and maybe are still there and, depending on the answer, can change the course of one's life forever.

Remember Your Values From Home

"Be my girl?" The sound of Eric's soft tenor voice played over and over again in Kim's mind. A wide grin spread across her face. "I finally got a beau", she thought. The previous evening's activities played over and over again like a 33 RPM stereo record: Eric coming over with the General tso's chicken;

the way he laid out the plastic ware on top of the neatly folded napkins, as well as the way he carefully spooned out the chicken and the yellow rice. "He has manners like my dad", Kim reminisced wistfully, remembering Paul. "I hope he'd meet my daddy's standards." Suddenly, Kim felt a lump in her throat and felt strangely sad. Lately, she found herself thinking a lot about Paul and their father-daughter conversations. She hungered for these connections as being away at college brings so many different life choices one has to make. Sometimes, just going from class to class on the crowded campus with thoughts of the course requirements; navigating the territory between street smarts and book smarts and learning to firmly set boundaries can make one feel both lonely and pressured at the same time. Kim found herself thinking about Paul played scenarios in her mind about what Paul would say about Eric if he were here.

"Young man, tell me about yourself. What is your course of study?"

"Well sir, I'm a political science major and____

"What politics is gonna change, they say the same thing in so many different ways and at the end of the day nothing has changed." (Paul had a tendency to ask questions and then cut people off in mid sentence to give his opinion.")

"Well sir, with all due respect, we have to form a party for the people and spread the wealth and_____")Paul would probably interrupt again).

"Spread wealth for who mon? They want you to think they're givin' you somethin' but at the end of the day, it's back in their pockets again mon."

Kim played the question and the debate scenario in her head, imagining Eric politely fielding her father's questions and statements while staying poised. Then, the questions and comments would come that were designed to make the young man sweat.

"So, you know me daughter from the university, no?"

"Yes sir."

"She's a good girl, she's my heart, you know."

"Yes sir."

"Tell me about your people. Where they from?"

(Kim imagined Paul studying Eric intently as he spoke, listening to every word and nuance. Paul knew at what point when to stop talking and interrupting and just listen and study. This came in handy for his work as a security guard. If only that night had turned out differently_). Kim felt her eyes fill with tears at the memory of Paul's violent death. Working to protect property just didn't seem to be worth it, if the ruling class was going to pocket the wealth anyway. Eric's socialist mindset was beginning to infiltrate Kim's thinking, and at the same time, she was really feeling the pain of losing her father in a real way. As a youngster, she was more interested in watching how her mama was going to cope; watching and hearing Gloria wail from her soul made Kim afraid that she was going to lose her mama too. Now on the cusp of womanhood, Kim felt the instinctive need of having a father figure to run to for protection.

Kim is in a place of contrasting choices: once again recognizing the joy of God's goodness; continuing on the path of truth that she was raised on, remembering Gloria' maxims and Paul's stories. On the other hand there is the definite lure of first love. At times, Kim felt as if she died and went to heaven, when she and Eric would sit together in the cafeteria and chat over dinner. He would carefully cut the dry pot roast that Kim had trouble cutting. He held utensils like a masterpiece and mastered them so skillfully. In any drama there is the conflict of good versus evil. *For we wrestle not against flesh and blood, but against principalities and powers.* There is a prize to be won. For virtue to be captured by evil, that is the prize of value. There is nothing to be gained, however, when good crosses over to the side of evil. It's like holding a cash award loosely and not making sure it's secure. When the contents fall, the one who finds it benefits, and the one who carried it loosely, loses. The dating game and the stock market are similar. In the stock market, there is the buy and sell price. How long does one hold on before they sell, If they sell too quickly they lose. In the dating game, how much of oneself does one give.? If one gives too much too soon, they lose.

**Point #1 Remember the good shepherd**

Kim decides to go to chapel service upon thinking about her dad. Somehow, being in a quiet place, reminiscing about life, a protective dad and a loving mom gave Kim the incentive to return to her first love. The stained glass windows allowed the sunshine to bathe the pews with a soft, warm glow. The hushed tones of worshippers kneeling by the pews, softly praying, lips moving, eyes closed, along with the soft sound of the pipe organ in the background gave the entire atmosphere a reverence that Kim realized she had been missing.

All That I AM

All that I am, all that I do
All that I ever have
I offer now to you
Take and sanctify these gifts
for your honour Lord
Knowing that I love and serve you
is enough reward
all that I dream All that I pray

all that I ever make
I give to you

Kim closed her eyes and swayed to the music. "Oh Lord" she thought, "I have been missing you." Kim arose from kneeling and turned to listen to minister Kent lead the worship service. He spoke from the book of Job chapter 28; In Praise of Wisdom was the title of the message. Minister Kent drew inferences from nature and creation, elaborating upon the intelligent design of a Creator who made so many living things, each with its own unique purpose. "For he looketh to the ends of the earth, and seeth under the whole heaven." He sees what you are thinking, my sister, my brother. He knows what you and I are wrestling with, and sees the weight we're carrying". At that point, Kim personalized the sermon and thought about the crossroads she now found herself in; living away from home, meeting new students, some from countries she only visited on a map; sharing a dorm room with a sharp, streetwise roommate and not wanting to appear out of the loop. To top it off, experiencing a soul tie with a young man that she met just weeks earlier in the library who asked her out. Now feeling desires to move beyond the safe place that she was raised to remain in, until the appropriate time.

At the conclusion of the service Kim exited the sanctuary with a renewed sense of purpose. There was a sense of getting her life's priorities in order. "They that wait upon the Lord shall renew their strength", Kim remembered Gloria's oft repeated favorite scripture when life's challenges became overwhelming after Paul's death. Strolling through the campus, Kim stopped and watched the Ohio State Buckeyes practice their warm ups. "That reminds me" Kim thought out loud, "physical fitness leads to mental alertness". She then walked over to the health and wellness center to find the schedule stating the days and times of the various fitness activities. The Red Cross blood drive was next Thursday. "Maybe I won't be as anemic as the last time", Kim thought. She jotted down the date and time of the cross training classes and the blood drive, and headed back toward her dorm room. Might as well try to pull up this GPA to at least a "B" Kim thought to herself, feeling a sense of restoration and purpose that she had not felt in a while.

**Point #2 Distractions take you away from your destiny**
Kim purposed in her heart to apply those principles that she was taught from home by her mom and dad. "It's true", Kim thought, "That which you hear over and over again becomes a part of you.

# A Fine Piece of Chocolate

The Buckeye state's Ohio State University campus was alive with a flurry of activity around the upcoming holiday season. Even Arneatha cut down on her jabs about Kim being a "goody two shoes." The festive decorations throughout the campus reflected the diversity of its students and created a sense of excitement within Kim. "I feel as if I belong now", Kim explained as she shared her testimony at the Fisher of men club. "Jesus wants us to be fishers of men, and I don't feel that little out of place feeling I sometimes felt when I first arrived on campus a little over three months ago." There were smiles and nods of affirmation and murmurs of "praise the Lord" and "amen" throughout the room in Emerson hall. The students played Yolanda Adams and Amy Grant CDs, as well as Asian songs sung in Chinese and Korean. The melody and harmony conveyed a peaceful, reverential tone. At the conclusion of the meeting, Kim strolled across the campus to her dorm room, humming Silent Night. A smiling Kim turns the lock to her dorm room, and her eyes immediately fall upon the half consumed beer bottles. Arneatha and her friends, some of whom were unfamiliar to Kim were seated around the small kitchen table amidst half consumed bottles of Coors beer. Arneatha immediately took note of the small bible in Kim's left hand and that she stopped smiling upon seeing the beer bottles.

"Well if it isn't Miss Righteous. Want some?" Arneatha held up an open bottle of Coors to Kim. Kim frowned and shook her head "no". "For real, you want some? seriously, I'm offering this to you, my friend." "Oh 'neatha, you see she doesn't want it", said a smiling young woman wearing a red head band over smoothly coiffed hair. "That's OK, it's cool. Nobody's gonna tell the preacher, or mom or dad____" Kim's eyes flashed angrily at the mention of the word, "dad" and said with a flash of boldness that surprised even her, "leave my dad out of this! OK? My dad died some years ago and there is no need to mention him like that, OK? A few murmurs of "I'm sorry" went around the room. Arneatha, having a few beers and an audience, couldn't afford to look chastised in front of her friends. "Yo, like, I didn't know it was like that with your dad. You never spoke of him before, so I just thought he was there and left."
"Well, he died and I don't want to talk about him now, OK?"
"Like I said, that's why you need some of this (holding up the bottle).
Kim (exasperated) "I said "no".
Arneatha (stepping close enough to Kim to the point where Kim could smell the alcohol on her breath) "Like I said, my bad, OK? I

know some of the righteous folk take their nip now and then, like that preacha whose church my aunt would take me and my sisters and brothers to. You could see the form of the flask underneath his jacket and he'd be up there shoutin' "halleleewyah" The girls laughed and howled at the parody the drunken Arneatha made about the preacher. Kim felt her face grow hot with embarassment. She turned away so they could not see the redness in her face and acted like she was surfing the refrigerator for something to eat, even though she was still full from the Fisher of Men Fellowship. Not wanting to appear bullied and defeated, Kim looked at her watch, stopped, feigned surprise, saying audibly, "oh my goodness, I forgot that (voice trailed off). Quickly she put on her coat and grabbed her keys—"be right back", and quickly left the room before anyone could ask questions. Anger rose up within Kim. "Why that stupid, arrogant fool", Kim thought. "I'm sick of her, just sick of her! The joy and revival of spirit that Kim felt just an hour ago was gone, completely gone. In its place was frustration and intense dislike of her roommate.

*Love your enemies. If your enemy slaps you on one cheek, offer him the other.*

The cold, late fall Ohio air left Kim feeling winded. She slowed down and reached into her coat pocket for her cellphone. She scrolled through her contact list and stopped for a second at her mom's #. She thought of calling Gloria at first to confirm her Amtrak reservations back to Newark Penn station and maybe vent about her roommate, but then she decided she could handle things herself, and call her next week. Kim scrolled further down until she reached Eric's number. Smiling, she punched in the digits. "Eric?" she heard him pick up. "Kim? How's my girl doin? (audible voices in the background) Eric, Hi, what's up? "Hold on, hon." (She heard him say something inaudible and there was some more talk and raucus laughter. Kim's heart sank. "You mean he's busy now?" Kim thought to herself. "I just want to talk to Eric 1:1.

Eric (back to the phone) "Yeah, hon, what's up?"

Kim "oh, I'm just out for a stroll, getting some cool air.

Eric—at this time of night? You better be careful.

Eric turned again to address whoever was in the background. Some more laughter and talking. "I'm sorry babe. What's up?

Kim (wistful tone to her voice) "Oh __ Eric. Just felt like calling."

Eric "you sure everything's OK?

Kim "yeah"

Eric—turning back to an audience at his end of the line "chill, keep it down".

Kim—who's that?

Eric—some of the guys from the Soul-A-Dad trio and The Vikings.

Kim—anyone I know?

Eric no, babe (Kim thought he sounded either somewhat evasive or maybe just distracted). "Hey girlfriend, let me call you back later, so I could spend some time with you."

Kim (dejected) Oohkay

Eric—what's the matter? (Turning to voices in the background) Like I said, I'll be with you in a minute"

Kim who was that?

Eric (softly so only Kim could hear) "uhmm, you are so sweet. I gotta call you back, girlfriend when it's just you and I. Love me?

Kim hesitated.

Eric—hey, you love me? (a little more urgently). "I love you." Kim felt a heart throbbing sensation go through her being at those last three words. "I love you too", she replied.

Eric—got to go. (hung up)

At that point, Kim felt a strange, agonizing disappointment engulf her being. It felt even like a sense of loss. She wondered, what else was going on that was making him so distracted.

*Can two walk together unless they be agreed? (Amos3:3)*


**Point #1 Stand your ground no matter what the distraction**

Kim continued walking until she found a clearing. She thought out loud herself about all that transpired earlier that evening: The fellowship with the Fisher of Men club, which rejuvenated her soul and helped her to focus on the one true Source of her happiness, and the joy just shattered within the space of an hour upon returning to her campus dorm room. Arneatha, like a cat waiting to pounce on its prey. *beware of your adversary like a roaring lion seeking whom he may devour.*

"Who is she anyway!" Kim thought, bringing up her mom and dad like that! "Oh daddy! Kim thought, stifling a sob. How she longed to hear her dad's rich Barbadian accent and feel his arm around her shoulder as they walked from Jim's candy store to buy Laffy Taffy. That was an occasional treat Paul allowed Kim to have. Paul wasn't big on indulging children with a lot of snacks. He believed that all of these indulgences not only rotted the teeth but corrupted the character. "And Eric, where were you? she mused out loud. I needed you to hear me out, say something to put things in perspective and you weren't even listening!"

At that point, Kim just sat and listened to the still sounds of the night, in the Columbus Ohio air. The stillness of the night and the coolness of the air was like a comforting blanket around Kim, with just the occasional sound of a car on the road in the distance. After kicking around some thoughts inwardly, thoughts of her first visit back to Newark, New Jersey since she left for college nearly four months ago, would the neighborhood seem different? Hopefully Gloria would still be getting more customers for her wellness business, especially at this time of the year. "Oh right!" Kim thought. "I was supposed to call Gloria and confirm the Amtrak departure on December 20th. All these distractions coming up all the time; I guess I need some down time with freshman seminar coffee club. Let me get back now." Kim realized she must have been sitting for a long time as she felt an ache in her gluteal muscles upon arising. Nevertheless, she felt more at peace, putting this evening's entire scenario into perspective.

**Point #2 Maintain the proper perspective, no matter what the situation**

Kim strode purposefully back in the direction of the dorm. She estimated she was about 1/2 or maybe a little less than 3/4 of a mile away from Archer hall. Having those quiet moments away from the crowds with its diversity of attitudes along with its diversity of people gave Kim the energy to regroup and gain back her sense of confidence and strength. She unlocked her dorm room and nodded and smiled briefly at Bridgette, who was the last of the trio of Arneatha's friends to leave. Kim's confidence radiated throughout the dorm room. "What up"? Bridgette said simply as she prepared to depart. Arneatha simply nodded, clicking the remote between BET, local Ohio News and some late night rerun of Law and Order. As Kim checked her cellphone clock she saw it was 11:30PM. She meant to call Gloria since early this week. "I guess it's not too late", Kim thought, since Gloria encouraged her daughters to "always call, no matter what, any time." The phone rang about five times, then Gloria answered. "Hi Mom!"
Gloria at first sounded groggy, and then became quickly animated at the sound of Kim's voice.
"Baby, is that you?"
"Yes mom, it's me."
"I called you, you know, and I sent you the letter, did you get it?:

"Yeah ma, I didn't forget. Just busy."

"Don't forget your Ma. I said, "Kim's all grown up and gone off to school; she's done forgot who her mama is (Kim cut in)

"I didn't forget. Listen, next week Tuesday I'll be catching the 5:17AM from Dayton and I should be in Newark by 1:19PM.

"Great!!" Gloria screeched in the phone. "Zodie, she's asleep now or I woulda gotten her up. Aunt May, she asks me about you. I said, I don't hear from her too much . . . How's the dorm? how's the roommate? Can you talk?"

Kim pursed her lips together and thought quickly. "It's all good. Everything is good. I think you would like her. Hey ma, I gotta go and finish this report; Keep up these grades you know. Love You! Give Zodie a kiss for me." Kim hung up before Gloria could make any more inquiries. She started filtering in her mind what she would say upon returning home and what details she would leave out regarding inquiries Gloria might make, especially where roommates and young men are concerned. Now, it's time to make a list and start packing.

**Point #3 New experiences give one new conflicts and choices**

As Kim packed, she wondered what her reaction would be to her neighborhood, after being away for four months, as well as conflicting emotions about Eric; wanting to be with him as his girlfriend and at the same time being painfully aware about Eric's lack of faith or interest in spiritual matters. The tension between Kim and Arneatha thawed over the next few days as much of the campus population was making plans preparing to leave for winter recess. The girls shared their plans for the upcoming holiday season. Arneatha would be visiting her aunt Cookie in Bed-Stuy Brooklyn. It seemed as if Cookie was the one who provided stability during Arneatha's tumultuous growing up years and encouraged her to leave the 'hood and go away to college. The fact that Arneatha was considering a profession as a social worker was somewhat surprising to Kim but then as she rethought it, it was not so surprising as people often choose professions that reflect their interests and obstacles they had to overcome early in life.

"So, who's that guy you been seeing" Arneatha asked. "He's into neo-soul?"

Kim spontaneously smiled. "Eric, his name is Eric Baines."

"Eric Baines. I could see you're sweet on him. Yeah, you go girl."

Kim giggled.

"So, what's he like?" Arneatha asked with a mischievous glint in her eye.

"He's neat, he's cool, he's charming".

"Oh come on. What's he like to go out with? to be with?"

Actually, they really hadn't been out on any real dates like the movies.

"And you been seeing him how long?" Arneatha probed.

"About a week after the BSU dance."

"That's been about a month now. You guys hang out?" (Kim felt a sense of rising impatience, but attempted to deflect it.)

"Hey, 'neatha, it's all good. I go and listen to his band, we talk, hang out. I'm studying, keeping up the grades while keeping it real, you know?" Kim hoped she sounded confident and cool enough.

"Well, keep it up, little Sis. Watch out for the groupies you know", Arneatha said dismissively.

"Ouch", Kim thought inwardly. Sometimes Arneatha had a way of saying things that felt like a punch in the stomach. The best way to deflect that was to act as if it didn't bother her. The comment gave Kim time to pause and think about her relationship with Eric. Sometimes he would call several times a day, pontificating about collectivist ideology and the importance of getting the masses to think as one and tax the elite until the wealth is spread among the masses. "This socialized health care will ensure that everyone gets equal health services", Eric said one evening while they were in the lounge, with his arm curved around her shoulder. Although the pose was cozy, sometimes it seemed as if Eric was in his own world listening to his own soapbox.

Kim desires to know Eric's true feelings for her. To the degree that this is important to her is the degree that Kim is falling deeper for him. Sometimes Eric said he would like to visit her in her dorm or in his dorm "where there's less distractions and we could talk one on one." Kim felt uneasy about the one on one since she wasn't sure how her growing feelings would lead her to respond to physical closeness. She also felt shy and awkward about socializing in her dorm room when Arneatha and her friends are around, listening to the two of them talking. "All this must be what the college advisor and her mom meant about making decisions on my own", Kim sighed.

Eric originates from Pittsburg, where his mother is a pediatric nurse and his father is partner in a law firm, "the only African American law firm successfully serving the downtown Pittsburg area, Eric would tell her proudly. "And his mom and dad each have their own car, with plans to get Eric his own car as long as he maintains at least a "B" average.

"I wish he would come down from Pittsburg by train or car to see me over this long holiday," Kim thought. Finally Eric calls on Monday, the 19th.

"How's my girl doing?"

"Oh, it's you, how are you doing?"

"What's up with, oh it's you? That's what my girl thinks of me? Eric said with a slight laugh.

"Seems like you've been missing in action,' Kim replied."

"I had to finish a poly-sci final and cut this CD. Oh man, my boys, they just need to focus . . .

Before Eric could continue stretching the conversation into a drawn out drama about his boys, something Kim didn't really want to hear, she decided to cut him off. (Sounding as if she's a police officer waving on traffic) "Attention, attention, I need you to focus on me, Eric Baines, me! your girl, remember? (brief pause; sound of silent surprise). Finally Eric said, "my baby, letting her man know what she needs. Hey, I like that."

"I mean it, Eric. Sometimes I feel as if I don't know where I stand with you. I know music is your heart, but sometimes I feel like you're not even with me. I just need to know how you really feel, Eric!

Kim stopped there. She heard her pitch rising and didn't want to appear too needy. "If only I didn't have that conversation with Arneatha," Kim thought regretfully. Some people just throw cold water on your dreams and want to mess up your good thing. The silence was a bit longer, as Eric for the first time was seeing Kim as a real woman with needs and a reasonable need for attention. Finally he speaks deliberately. "Kim, babe, you are my heart, you're my girl. You're special to me and I need you to be there for me, as I am there for you."

Kim, (voice softening). "I know. I'm going home tomorrow to see my folks. Be back on the sixth."

As Eric didn't volunteer his plans Kim asked hopefully, "so what are your plans?

"Well, I'll be here celebrating Kwanzaa and then I'll be headed towards Pittsburg on the 27th and meet you back on campus on the sixth.

"Oh", Kim said, sounding crestfallen. (Another uncomfortable silence. She was secretly hoping that Eric would be available at least part of the holiday and perhaps surprise her with a gift like a gold chain, or something that symbolized their link.

"Hey Kim", said Eric. "How about postponing the trip until the 23rd, and we could hang out. I'll treat you to BBQ's in Dayton, and you could still be with your folks before Christmas. One on one time, you and I."

A wave of emotions engulfed Kim, but she knew she would lose ground if she acted needy. "I just thought my guy wanted to be with me over recess, that's all."

Oh Kim," I like you a lot. I really do. Hey, I know now I've been busy, way too busy. That's no way to treat my girl. (pause) "Hey, I got another idea. When is that train leaving tomorrow? 5:17AM/ hey, let me treat you to that jazz supper club and we could listen to Miles, Count Basie and some old school R&B.

"Sounds good." Kim's tone instantly brightened.

"Yeah, I definitely got to do right by my girl this time."

"This time?" (Kim wondered for a second). Eric's voice broke into Kim's thoughts. "Pick you up tonight at 7.

"OK.

Kim signed off and went through her closet, looking for something that would grab Eric's attention.

"Eric's a cool guy. I hope I could get into his heart and he could understand me as I try to understand him."

An age old question is, "is the cup half empty or half-full". Kim has her man in one sense, but on the other hand he has his goals that sometimes excludes her. When she's with him, the cup is half full. When she's not with him, the cup is half empty. Which half of Eric is Kim really experiencing? Only time will tell.

# A Fine Piece of Chocolate

Can two walk together unless they be agreed? (Amos 3:3)

When two people are each on a different spiritual plane, they are really flying on different altitudes, even if it appears as if they are one. For Kim, faith, family, and success in school are competing with a whole host of academic and moral choices. Study, then distractions, then get back to studying later. Kim is idealistic, bright, and raised in the security of a Christian home with two loving parents until the murder of her dad at age twelve. Kim, while stunned, did not give vent to her feelings as Gloria, with the support of her family, Paul's family, as well as kind neighbors, loaned the support they needed. Gloria was ambitious: she worked full time at the boutique and continued to build up her wellness business, as well as nurturing her girls.

Eric is bright, clever, and a bit of a party animal. Erudite and attractive, he has the makings of a politician. The world, as far as he's concerned, is made up of the masses and the much smaller (and wiser) ruling crowd. While he appeals to the masses with his power to the people mindset, he looks to reign in a seat of power. His elitist drive leads him to give people what they want so that he can get to where he needs to go.

As unlikely as the coming together as these two seem to be, there is nothing like chemistry.

*Chemistry—that elusive coming together of two kindred souls. It cannot be described but when it is present, it's evident.*

Chemistry creates the rhythm of a fast heartbeat anticipating what's next. We give chemistry a name. We call it "love", and love has a tendency to heighten our senses.

### Point #1 Desires determine our reality, whether it is really real or not.

*Setting: Kim is poring over her wardrobe, trying to put together the right texture of color, flair, and a bit of seduction. "Not too much" as Gloria would admonish. She was glad she had the room to herself, with no witty smart tongued roommate to give her suggestions. "It's biting tonight, so I better wear these gloves", Kim thought aloud as she pulled out a pair of winter white knit gloves, along with the ruffled blouse which showed a bit of decolletage and the blue skinny jeans. "The freshman 15 didn't creep up on me yet", Kim smiled to herself. The tan suede pantcoat Kim bought at Marshall's gave just the right balance to her lean frame. The Revlon lipstick and Maybelline foundation with the turquoise and sand eyeshadow gave Kim's countenance a more worldly projection than what she actually* possessed. *"Maybe that's why Gloria limited Kim's experimenting with makeup to lipstick and one pastel eyeshadow when she was allowed to date"* Kim wondered. *"But anyway, tonight's the night I go out with my boo."*

At 7:20PM, Eric rang the doorbell to Kim's dorm. *"The politician in him is running late, collecting votes maybe?"* Kim thought sarcastically to herself, her enthusiasm dampened somewhat by Eric's tardiness. However when she opened the door her mood changed instantly. Wearing jeans and a blue suede coat and tan suede boots, Eric greeted her with his right hand extended, holding out a single red rose. "For the lady". Kim moved right past the rose and wrapped her arms around Eric's slim waist, giving him the most enthusiastic, open mouthed kiss she ever gave anyone. *"He tastes so sweet"*, Kim thought; *"sweet as honey"*. That emotion we call love has a tendency to heighten our senses. If it has a taste, it's sweet as sugar. If it has sight, love is so fine it's larger than life, and when it comes to hearing, nothing makes the ears tingle at the sound of the lover calling the loved one's name. *"Kim"* Eric murmured in Kim's ear as he broke the prolonged kiss. *"I love you, you know?"* Kim squeezed her eyes tight as she was beginning to get teary eyed and a bit overwhelmed. *"No one ever said this to me before."* The atmosphere was so charged, it felt like an out of body experience to Kim. *"Dear God, please understand and let it be true"*, Kim pleaded silently to God about her relationship to Eric. They held on tight to each other, bathed in the aura of each other's presence. Eric glanced down at his watch and announced, *"we better get moving, hon or we'll miss dinner tonight, unless of course you'd prefer to order in. Whatever the lady wants,"* he winked.

*"Oh no, we better get moving"* Kim laughed, as they headed out of Archer Hall and walked toward West Lane Avenue to catch the bus to Dayton. They stood huddled together against the early winter chill waiting for the bus in a mutually comfortable silence. As they boarded the bus they were lucky enough to get two seats together and enjoy the hour long ride. Finally Eric said "babe, take off these gloves. I want to feel your hand." Kim answered, "I'm wearing them cause they match my outfit but, if you say so." Upon clasping Eric's right hand with her left hand, Kim felt an aura go up her left arm. Momentarily she was transfixed into the future with Eric, walking along the beach, sitting together in church (oh how she wished) and maybe, just maybe, standing at the altar, the way her mom and dad did when her mom was 22 and her dad was 32. The scene

was so mesmerizing that for a few moments she lost track of time, and it wasn't until she heard the commanding voice of Eric calling her name that she was startled to attention. "What's the matter? I called you three times. Is something the matter?'

"Oh no".

"Sure?"

"Yeah, it's so pretty this time of the year; kinda reminds me of home" Kim said, hoping to deflect Eric's probing.

"Miss your folks?"

"Kind of".

"Well, maybe one day I'll meet them".

A broad grin broke out across Kim's face. "Yeah, that'll be great!" Eric (in a low voice). "I knew you'd like that."

Kim (thinking to herself) "I wonder what he means by that?" but then her attention quickly shifted to a marching band playing some festive music that she wasn't familiar with. The retail stores dotted the Columbus landscape with displays of the Nutcracker, Santa Claus, unique window displays and a few nativity scenes. All this reminded Kim of the occasional visits that she, her mom and sister would take to 5th Avenue in New York City. It was a happy yet poignant memory. At last they reached their destination.

Dayton's BBQ flashed green and red all around the perimeter entrance. As Eric and Kim entered the restaurant the atmosphere was festive. There was a Santa Claus in one corner, and a moosehead with huge antlers perched over the entryway leading to the bar. There was a prominent sign that read, **"No one under 21 served. Show ID.** Kim inadvertently pulled back upon seeing the sign. Eric turned around and smiled, taking Kim's hand and saying, "come on babe, it's OK. They gotta post that for legal purposes. No one's checking anyway."

"Yeah but" Eric silenced Kim's protestings with a kiss. They proceeded to the bar where Eric took a menu on laminated paper that had different categories of beer, wine and spirits.

*Wine is a mocker, strong drink is raging; and whosoever is deceived thereby is not wise. Proverbs 20:1*

The bar was crowded and Eric gave Kim the one available seat around the counter. "You could have a non alcoholic also known as a *virgin* cocktail" Eric said with the emphasis on the word, "virgin". Kim wasn't sure if Eric was being sarcastic or not. "I really never drank before but, she added quickly, I would like to have a bite to eat first."

"Oh yeah, well here's a food menu." Eric handed her a menu that had mainly appetizers. Kim felt vaguely disappointed as her idea of a first date to a restaurant would be sitting in a booth with a nice centerpiece and being waited on by an attentive waiter working for his or her tip. However, she didn't verbalize any of this.

Eric, noting Kim's discomfort sitting at the bar, began expounding upon the benefits of beer drinking. "It contains vitamin B-6 and makes the hair shine."

"If I want all that I can take a vitamin pill" Kim responded.

Undeterred, Eric continued. "It even has antioxidants. In ayurvedic therapy, it is known to relax one and reduce stress. Hey, the wise soul relaxes to clear the mind."

Kim didn't want to let on that she didn't know anything about ayurvedic therapy and never heard of it. "Well, we all have to relax", Kim laughed. "I'm just getting really hungry, that's all."

"OK, what would you like to order?" Eric asked as he held up the menu for her to see better in the dimmed light. Kim ordered salmon croquettes and a small garden salad with house dressing. Eric ordered a sub sandwich with roastbeef and melted cheese. A swirl of thoughts enveloped Kim's mind. "Is this what dating in college is about? Should I want more? Maybe I need to just give it time to grow. Yeah, that's what I'll do."

As soon as the seat next to Kim was vacated, Eric sat next to Kim, in time for the waiter to bring both plates. They ate in silence among the festive, and at times loud chatter. Finally Eric broke the silence by stating to Kim that he didn't want her to be uncomfortable, but he wanted them to enjoy the atmosphere before Kim has to return to campus and leave in the morning.

"Sounds good", Kim answered.

"You're okay?" Eric asked.

"Yeah, I'm good."

Eric placed his arm around Kim's shoulder and asked her what she would like to drink.

**Point #2 Recognize and beware of the idols in your life**

Idolatry as practiced first starts with a desire for an object, being a thing or a person, even a concept. Kim struggles in part to stay in the good graces of a streetwise roommate instead of being concerned about what does God think. Idolatry is subtle, as it incrementally draws the heart of its victim into the arms of the object of its affection. Kim is drawn to Eric, knowing he's not walking in the same path as she is. He says and does the right things and presto! she wants him. It's also true that one's environment can have a greater impact on a person's choices than they realize. Eric, who is an aspiring politician will say and do whatever it takes to get Kim to yield to him. Now, back to the story.

"Here's a suggestion, Kim. I know a very mild drink that really has no liquor at all."
"Really? What's it called?"
"A pomegranate cosmopolitan drink, which has, as its main ingredient suggests, the pomegranate fruit. It has lemon juice and just a touch of orange liqueur (*holding his thumb and index finger together, to emphasize how little the liqueur is*). "Just a flavor enhancer to downplay the acid in the fruit and bring out the sweet taste." (*Eric conveniently leaves out the fact that it has vodka in it*).
"I'm not really sure, as long as it isn't really a *real* drink."
"It's not bad, trust me."

Eric calls the bartender over and orders two pomegranate cosmopolitan drinks. "A little extra orange liqueur for the lady. (Eric knew Kim liked sweets, and the orange liqueur would blunt the taste of the vodka.) Soon Kim relaxed in Eric's embrace, and the artists performing for the evening entertainment began performing.
A large, heavy set lady named Big Eva sang several Ella Fitzgerald songs. A Tisket A Tasket was a hit with the over 50 crowd. She strained to hit the high notes, and the audience clapped politely for her efforts. "Oh come on, you could do better than that. Give another round of applause to Big Eva!!

A local, youthful group played some instrumental hits by Booker T and the MGs, then a Latin band played some Santana and Mongo Santamaria hits. Eric let out a yell in appreciation of the songs. Kim felt somewhat embarassed, but she noticed people around the table hollered back in agreement. Kim found herself feeling more relaxed than she's ever been. It was becoming difficult to stay awake. Eric was more loud and vocal than she remembered seeing him. The music seemed to have had him in a trance. Finally the DJ announced the last song for the evening. "Ladies, this is especially for you. Have you ever had a man who was convicted? found guilty? (a few low murmurs of "yeah, uh-huh.) What if he had to stand before the judge because he's standing accused of loving you?" Right then a tall cocoa brown muscular gentleman wearing black leather trousers and a tank top, a smooth dome and a beard, a dead ringer for Isaac Hayes, began in a low voice singing

"I stand accused of Loving You. This brought back memories to Kim of Gloria listening to some old school R&B when she had time after putting in an eight, sometimes 10 hour day at the boutique. Kim felt a mixture of gut level homesickness and at the same time a certain level of comfort and exhaustion, a mixture that was hard to describe. Eric put his arm around Kim's shoulder, squeezing her. A part of her really did not want to leave. "Come on boo I see someone's getting sleepy."

**If it's love, he will look out for you**

Kim reluctantly arose but Eric told her to wait while he goes to the ticket area to pick up their coats. As they left and braved the winter night's chill, arms wrapped around each other, Kim stumbled several times, not sure if it was the sidewalk or something in her drink. The logistics of getting back to Columbus started turning nightmarish as upon reading the schedule at the bus stop it seemed as if the buses stopped running after midnight. The only other bus service was local service that wasn't always reliable. Eric checked his wallet to see if he could manage a gypsy cab back to Columbus. "Babe, how about if we go dutch this time?" Eric said as he looked in his wallet. Kim was somewhat crestfallen as her idea of a date did not involve putting out cash for any of the expenses. "Just this time", Eric pressed. "This usually doesn't happen to me but hey, I wanted to show you a good time before you go back east to see your folks." Kim reluctantly fishes through her purse and hands Eric a $20 bill. "I need to get back in time to take the campus shuttlebus to the train station. I could try to get three hours of sleep before I have to get up and take the shuttlebus over." Just then Eric waved down a gypsy cap and haggled him down for a reasonable fare. (Turning to Kim, smiling) "See, I wouldn't leave my boo hanging like that. I got all the bases covered".

"Daddy took care of everything when he took mom out," Kim thought as she and Eric entered the backseat. "I guess this is dating 21st century style". That thought made going dutch a bit more bearable for Kim, as she snuggled up to Eric and dozed off. (An hour later Kim groggily woke up to the sound of Eric's persistent, "Kim, Kim, we're home baby, wake up!" It was the middle of the night and the cold air felt like an arctic blast. Kim immediately became fully alert. She and Eric walked briskly towards Archer Hall. It was nearly 2AM. As they walked towards Kim's dorm room they slowed down.

"Baby, it was great spending time with you before you catch the train back east to Newark."

"Yeah, Eric, I had fun too."

"Bet we could have more fun(unintelligible) Kim thought Eric murmured something about a midnight snack. Eric softly kissed Kim on her forehead, nose and neck. He ran the tip of his tongue down her neck that made her squeal "oh Eric stop! I gotta get some rest before I catch that bus in a couple of hours." Eric placed both of his hands on the wall over Kim's head. He gazed at her intently, not saying anything. She clenched the keys in her right hand and averted his intense gaze, feeling somewhat self-conscious.

"Well Eric, I need to say goodnight and catch a little rest." Finally Eric spoke, sounding as if he was measuring his words carefully. "You're special, Kim. You're different to a lot of girls on campus. (pause) "You mean a lot to me. I never met a girl quite like you before and I had to make you my girl." And with that statement he lowered his face into her face and gave her a gentle, yet passionate kiss that felt as if their two souls were merging into one entity. They released from each other. "Bye sweet" Eric said as he turned to walk down the hall and toward the exit. Kim stood and watched until Eric was out of sight.

### Coffee black or with cream?

*"Ah! How sweet coffee tastes. Lovelier than a thousand kisses, sweeter than muscatel wine." Johann Sebastian Bach*

Most people who drink coffee, including myself, enjoy the beverage because it is stimulant. Some of us like Bustelo or espresso, so powerful it is nothing but raw strength. Others prefer a mild, Dunkin' donuts type that is almost bland. While some like their coffee black, many prefer it with cream. Cream adds a mellowness to tone down the strength and the bitterness somewhat. The cream itself adds its own flavor. Relationships can be like that cup of coffee, with or without cream. The two people who make up that cast of characters called a relationship bring their own flavors as they merge into oneness.

Eric Baines is a man about town, who has made the use of words an art form. Having a worldly wise dad that's partner in the only minority owned law firm in the lower Pittsburgh area with a large and diverse clientele, makes the Baines family stand out in both the black community and the Pittsburgh community at large. Eric is used to being around people that take charge and promote a confident exterior. Visiting his dad's company and being around the array of clients his the law firm served piqued young Eric's desire for influence and power. Eric admired his dad and emulated his vocabulary and took to heart the manner in which his dad schooled him to "look them right in the eye" as he would at the same time clasp their hand with both of his upon greeting. "Son, you never know what someone can do for you in this business. Above all, listen and observe carefully, for you can craft a situation to get just what you need from anybody." Eric Sr. successfully represented buyers and sellers in disputed real estate transactions. He had an innate ability to see through and grasp the need of the individual, an art form that Eric Jr. picked up rather early in life. He picked up on the touches and glances from the women who worked in his dad's law firm, never quite sure which was just an office flirtation for which was something more. However things were, Eric Sr. was a man who maintained control in all situations. Hence, Eric Jr. knew how to adjust to situations and be as a strong cup of black coffee or mellow with cream.

Ultimately , ladies in a situation with such a man need to know what they want as if they do not control the situation, the situation will control them. When the situation is out of control, one finds out, like a cup of black coffee with no mellowness of cream, and the half full jar that feels fully empty, that two cannot walk together except if they agree.

# There's No Place Like Home

Home, sweet home: Kim was experiencing such a flurry of mental energy from last night's activities that, in her words: "It was all I could do to force myself to get three hours of sleep before I wake up too late and miss my train. After tossing and turning for what seemed like a catnap, the alarm clock rang shrilly in Kim's ear, causing her to literally jump out of her bed hurriedly wash up and dress before catching the campus shuttle bus to the Amtrak at Dayton. The red capped train attendant smiled as Kim awkwardly pulled her suitcase toward the train car steps, and, without a word, pulled the rolling suitcase up the steps and found a safe place for her luggage where it would be out of the way. The ticket clerk punched a hole in her ticket after she got seated, and this time, sleep overtook her.

The Amtrak sped quickly through the towns and villages from Midwestern Ohio until it reached its final destination of Newark Penn Station. "Newark Penn Station, last stop! Last stop! Everybody get off! The conductor projected his voice over and over again through the loudspeaker. Kim awakened, yawned, and stretched, squinting from the early afternoon sun. The kindly ticket clerk once again helped her pull her bulky luggage don the train car steps and unto the platform. "Thank you", Kim said politely. For a moment it felt like a bit of culture shock, being back in the big city. Huge crowds of people from all over the planet, it seemed, waiting for their loved ones. A large Hispanic family that appeared to be three generations got off the train and greeted family and friends with an anticipation worthy of someone who has been out of their lives for a long, long time. A tall, stately young man in an air force uniform was greeted by a young woman, perhaps a wife, perhaps a fiancée with a great big wrap around his neck hug and kiss. Kim felt a momentary wince at that sight. "Where are my people?" she thought. "I did tell Mom for her to meet me at 1pm near the upstairs seating area. After waiting for what seemed like an interminable period, Kim saw, in the distance the figure of her Mom, a little heavier than she was before Kim left. "It looks as if Gloria put on the freshman 15 for me," Kim thought. "There's Kim! My big Sis! Zodie hollered out, sounding a bit younger than her twenty years. Immediately she pulled out a banner, along with Gloria holding it up. With gold and red glittering on a green background were the words emblazoned, "Welcome home, Kim." Kim was instantly touched to the point of feeling her eyes water. "Thank you Lord, for my wonderful mom and sister," she thought.

"There's my baby!" Gloria shouted. The three members of the Smith clan laughed, hugged, and laughed some more. "Sorry we were late, baby," Gloria explained. There was just so much traffic, stops and starts with the cab. I almost thought we would never get here. Come on baby, let me help you with this, Gloria said, grabbing the belt of Kim's heavy luggage, and pulling it towards the exit. As the automatic doors opened and the early winter wind hit their faces, a Desius and Weslande green cab, a familiar form of transportation in Newark, honked at Gloria, Kim and Zodie. Gloria smiled and thanked him for being there right when she needed him. The cabbie hoisted Kim's large rolling suitcase into the back of the cab, returned to the driver's seat and asked, "where to?" "Two sixty five Ashland Avenue," Gloria replied. And off he sped into the traffic. Last minute holiday shoppers, crowding the streets, hoping to catch a sale for themselves or their loved ones. Young men hawking wares: CDs and DVDs, bootlegged movies, hoping to earn enough to buy their own gifts for their moms and baby mamas. Downtown Newark was abuzz with activity. Music stores were playing a combination of hip hop Christmas tunes and old school favorites like Nat King Cole's Merry Christmas. "Chestnuts roasting on an open fire; Jack Frost nipping at your nose . . . although it's been said, many times, many ways, Merry Christmas, to you."

The familiar sights of the playground, with groups of pre-K and kindergartners playing, under the watchful eyes of their caregivers, let Kim know that she was almost home. Just then the cabbie rounded the corner and pulled up to 265 Ashland Place. Gloria thanked him, tipped him $5 over the fare. "Thanks ma'am, thank you very much," he gushed. "Well, God has been good to me and my family," Gloria responded. "He gave my baby traveling mercies on her way home from college," motioning towards Kim. "Congratulations young

41

lady", the cabbie said, looking genuinely impressed. At that moment, Kim realized how important her success was to Gloria, and she made a mental note not to let her down. They waited for the forever slow elevators in the high rise. When it arrived they boarded and pressed 9, then walked to apartment 9G.

The time to spend with that sister circle of family and friends is a time to release stress. How do you release stress when the recurring thoughts keep pressing to the conscious? For a young sista being away for the first time in such an atmosphere of change, stress, is a given. To feel the pangs of love and desire conflicting with the purity she was raised with, that is stress. How does one release stress, given all of these changes?

### There's no place like home

"Kim, don't be traveling the world out here just 'cause you got back home for Christmas break. The world isn't what it used to be. You and Zodie going all over the place—" oh ma, don't worry, Kim said, reaching across the table, taking her mother's hand. I wouldn't go too far, just being away at Ohio state is far away from home for me. "(pause) what's the plans, Ma? Kim said with a twinkle in her eye. Gloria loved to entertain family and friends whenever the holidays arrived, or when any situation presented itself for celebration. The scent of the evergreen in the livingroom, the cinnamon candle, all worked together to create an atmosphere of love.

## A Fine Piece of Chocolate

### The support network of sister friends

To be 18 again. What does it mean to be 18? Is it the right to vote? The right to get away from your parents? The right to become a woman by experiencing a man? Just what is this thing called being 18?

### Choices

That's what it's about—the vast array of choices—what college should I go to? Should I stay home or go away? What about the majors and the minors? Friends? Networking, hookups and breakups. All these are the composite of being 18. Being 18 means choices, choices and more choices. Is it fair to have so much to choose from? Should I make all of these choices on my own? All of the humanistic professors say I am my own person. John Lennon said "Imagine there's no heaven. It's easy if you try."

### Waiting for him to call: Is it worth the wait?

One thing women today have lost, for the most part, is the art of the chase. If you watch a hunter go hunting, he has a specific prey in mind. He'll wear a certain camouflage in order to sneak up on the prey. If he's a fisherman he'll bait the hook for the specific fish and the key is, he'll wait. And that, ladies, is what too many of us forget to do. Why didn't you wait? 'cause, you were looking for love. Waiting—it's maddening, isn't it? Sometimes we as women go through our day, waiting for that phone call: can't even fully enjoy that day we were blessed to wake up and see.

Kim is in two places at once: reconnecting with her mom and sister Zodie, and with the friendly neighbors that drop by. What is the missing link? Eric. It's been almost 24 hours now. Where's the phone call. "Should I sneak and call him?" (Kim thinks to herself. "maybe he'll text me. Just keep smiling for every body. After all, its been the first time back home from college in four months. The atmosphere is so festive. People on the street are more friendly and engaging with each other. Gloria's network of sister friends are calling and stopping by. (Mrs. Hennessy stops by in her large overcoat and oversized hat, accentuating her large frame. "Baby! You're back, and look how you grew up. You are such a lady, Kim. "Hey, lady! (Mrs. Hennessy screeches a tad too loudly to Gloria as she peers into the apartment, then she looks back at Kim.) "Kim, you don't know how your mama worries, thinks and prays about you so much. Girl, you are blessed." (Mrs. Hennessy circles around Kim, admiring her hairstyle and the boucle style jacket she's wearing. "Such a lady you are. You bring style to Ohio State." At that remark, Kim broke out in a big grin.

Truly, there's nothing like that network of sister friends who know how to give that reassuring good word in season: that word that says everything will be allright and you believe it. When that moment of connection happens, the previous worries all seem minor. And you know why? There is nothing like one sister encouraging another sister whether she is a peer, a mother in the community, or a stranger who gives you a knowing smile. Throw in a major holiday like the Christmas season, the brother who is missing in action or doesn't call when expected can even be forgotten for a moment.

It's now 2pm, the day before Christmas eve. Kim decided to stop checking her text messages and looking back at placed and received calls, especially those from Eric. "Oh well," Kim sighed—"he did say he's call, and since he is my boo I could call or text him later. In the meantime, time to have fun with my folks." All along Central Avenue and cutting into Irvine Turner Blvd and Martin Luther King Jr. Blvd, the streets were alive with the anticipation over the Christmas holiday. Zodie couldn't wait to show Kim where she was taking vocational training, so the two of them boarded the 21 bus to downtown Newark to check out the at once familiar places, and yet feeling strangely outgrown from it all. Zodie had to show Kim the vocational training center where she received a certificate for office assistant, having learned Microsoft office, and learned to mail merge documents. Kim realized this made Zodie feel as if she accomplished success in her life as well. "And Kim," said Zodie, "the teacher had to go over that mail merge thing, you know, and I got it on the *second* try". Zodie sounded a bit loud and Kim whispered, "well, you know Zodie, as mom said, "God gave everybody their gifts and I guess you got yours."

The two young women got off to enjoy some lunch fare at Chuck E. Cheese. The store must have just opened, Kim thought, as she hadn't remembered one in this location. Kim wasn't one for a lot of fast food, but it was good connecting with her sister again. Couples walked along the busy streets, arm in arm, all in a world of their own. A tall slender young man and woman brushed past them. The woman's outfit bore some resemblance to the outfit Kim wore the night she and Eric went out to Dayton's BBQ. Without realizing it, Kim stopped suddenly and turned to watch them. "Who's that?" Zodie asked curiously when she saw Kim stop and watch them. "Oh, I thought I knew one of them at first, that's all", Kim lied mildly, trying to sound as casual as possible, then changing the subject.

The two sisters walked back to Martin Luther King Jr. Blvd and caught the 21 bus home, both sitting together but in two different worlds; Zodie, captivated by the day's events of having lunch with her big sis and seeing a movie, and Kim fantasizing about when she sees Eric again, even feeling the desire to consummate the relationship with Eric. "Is that what love feels like?" thoughts of the beloved creating a tingling sensation in the hands, a tension in the loins and the increase in the rhythm of the heartbeat. At the same time there is the nostalgia of home sweet home; Mom's cooking; neighbors and relatives stopping by, amazed at the poise and the womanliness of Kim, yet expecting nothing less as time goes on.

# Waiting as Preparation for the next event

As Shakespeare said, "All the world is a stage, and all the men and women are merely players.

Kim is waiting, with the typical measure of youthful impatience, to find out what this thing called love is. Love is waiting impatiently for that phone call from that special someone; waiting impatiently to see them again and fall into their arms.

What am I waiting for? is the impatient cry of the young and the restless. To those in that phase I will say, lovingly, "find yourself in this waiting period. This is the season that can make you or break you for the rest of your life. The foundation is being laid for subsequent life relationships. Ask yourself, young person, the following questions:

1) What goals should I set for my life?
2) Is this person I'm traveling with for now going to be there for me later?
3) Is this a worthwhile wait or is this going to be a waste?

Use this preparation wisely.

## You Must Have Faith

*Scene—It is the day before Christmas eve, and it is a flurry of activity at Gloria's house—The last minute touches to the black fruitcake that Gloria baked for when Paul's folks come by to celebrate; the wrapping of gifts, some of them secretly and outside the view of the recipient. In the midst of all of this activity the question is: Where will this young woman turn? faith or the flesh.*

Ace Johnson, the UPS driver who remembered Kim as a little girl, rings the bell and, with a sense of humor he is known for, gasps, eyes wide with surprise as he hands her the package. "Who is this woman? Kim, is that you? Wow!" He claps the palm of his hand to his forehead. I must've gotten stuck in a time machine. How's college?" "Fine," Kim answered somewhat self consciously . "Your parents got plenty to be proud of. Here, Merry Christmas, Happy Kwanzaa, all those good things. Tell Gloria I wish her a happy holiday."

Just then, Gloria exited from the bedroom, adjusting a false eyelash. "Who was that?" she asked, before whisking the heavy package out of Kim's arms and returning to her room. Kim's curiosity was piqued for a minute, but then interrupted by the telephone.

## Self Confidence

Weaning one's dependence away from one's parents and learning to make decisions for one's life involves development of self-confidence which impacts all life decisions, good and bad.

## What is Self-Confidence?

According the psychosocial theorist, Erik Erikson, all humans must pass through 8 stages of life from birth to late adulthood, in order to become fully functioning. Erikson coined the term, "Identity Crisis," which is a turning point in human development where the young person has to reconcile themselves with who they are and the person society expects them to become. This emerging personality will be established by forging past experiences with anticipations of the future. Ie. The crossroads of life. How will Kim reconcile the righteous teachings she was brought up with, with the longings of first love towards someone who may be questionable.

## Seize the moment

Right now is where anyone will ever be. The past is done, the future we can only imagine and manipulate in our minds. "Zodie!" Gloria called, "let me fix that, Gloria re buttoned the buttons on Zodie's collar. Gloria still gave her daughters the once over look before they exited the house together. First Corinthian Baptist Church is a sanctuary for the faithful who, through the vicissitudes of life, know the One by whom their help cometh.

The minister of music led the choir through a rendition of Highway to Heaven. "It's a Highway to heaven, none can walk up there, but the pure in heart. It's a highway to heaven, going up the king's highway." Kim, Gloria, and Zodie took their seats, third row from the front. Parishioners who hadn't seen Kim in a long time turned around, shook hands, gave Kim a warm hug. On the stage the little ones began filing in, the Babes for Christ Infant choir, decked out in their silver shiny caps, fashioned in the shape of a star. "Sister Pam certainly has an artistic flair and lots of patience," Kim thought, to fashion these hats for 40 children." Two of the little ones in the front of the line wore somber expressions as they walked in side by side, softly banging the drums with the drumsticks to The Little Drummer Boy as sister Pam mouthed the words and moved her hands rhythmically; the audience chuckling to the rumpuhpumpums. Teens for Christ and the Young Adults Moving Mountains did a moving play based upon the book of Luke, with Sister Jones' daughter, Sahara, playing the role of Elizabeth, Mary's cousin and Sister James's son playing the role of John. "It seemed as if they grew up overnight," Kim thought. Two new members played the role of Mary and Joseph, and the beautiful, chocolate colored baby doll was so authentic it appeared as if he would open his eyes and gurgle any moment.

Luke 1:50 "And his mercy is on them that fear him from generation to generation", the voice boomed from behind the curtain. "Oh, how I need you sometimes, Lord" Kim thought. Kim's attention shifted momentarily to the newly engaged couple, Jesse Wagner and his fiancée, Pauline. Jesse came from an accomplished family of educators and lawyers. "He just passed his bar exam and has his pick of law firms to make partner with" Gloria whispered to Kim. Jesse's right arm cradled protectively around Pauline. "Oh wow," Kim thought, "if only . . . I wish . . ." Just then, the audience broke into an applause and Kim stood up, joining in the applause of the congregation at the end of the first act when the character of Zacharias, young elder Thomas, who often spoke with a speech impediment spoke with perfect clarity, and not referring to any notes. "Blessed be the Lord God of Israel, for he has visited and redeemed his people, and hath raised up a horn of salvation for us in the house of his servant, David, that we should be saved from our enemies, and from the hand of them that hate us. To perform the mercy promised tour fathers . . . That he would grant unto us, that we being delivered out of the hand of our enemies, might serve him without fear, in holiness and righteousness before him, all the days of our life." (Luke 1:68-75)

"Bless him, Lord, bless him," shouted a tall sister in the front." "Jesus is in the house, whoo, whoo, whoo shouted a group of teens in the middle rows. And in that sacred moment, the all consuming love of God filled the atmosphere, so much so that nothing else on this side of eternity mattered.

## A Lesson of Values (Take Your Values With You)

Bishop McKinley, a large, imposing man mounted the pulpit, praising the Youth Department for their fine renditions of traditional Christmas music, read some last minute announcements, and then began his sermon. Bishop McKinley had a preaching style that was part narrative, "to make sure people get the location of the Word, as the Bible is the believer's road map," and then part expository.

"And let us turn to John chapter one. In the beginning was the Word, and the Word was with God, and the Word was God . . . And the Word was made flesh and dwelt among us . . ." After thoroughly giving the biblical background of Jesus' role as the Word, and his earthly parent's humble background, Bishop McKinley began an expository of poverty being tough, but yet character building.

"And in our time, young people jump da' broom before they jump da' broom (congregation gives a knowing chuckle). Was a time when if you were po' ya mama and ya daddy would warn ya to watch the company that ya' keep, cause the only thing ya have to lose is your name. Nowadays young people make a name for themselves with tattoos, piercings, imitate Biggie and Beyonce, (laughter). At least Beyonce said, "put a ring on it." Amen.

"OK, get on with the message please," Kim thought, feeling a rising sense of irritation. Almost on cue Pastor McKinley said, "anyway, back to the message. Joseph and Mary, like many young people, had their hopes and dreams. They were waiting for the messiah and living in perilous times, like many people today. They were poor but pure. They followed the commandments of God and although an engagement in Jewish culture was as binding as marriage, they were saving themselves for the wedding day, amen. Joseph loved Mary, and his natural instincts as a man of the Hebrew culture was to provide for and protect his wife. Imagine then, the confusion he felt when Mary told him she was with child. We know Joseph was righteous because nothing was said about him pointing at Mary and accusing her of infidelity, amen. The Word says that Joseph planned to put her away privately. He wasn't going to air their linen in public. He was a private man. See, brothers and sisters, God does everything decently and in order. Jesus the Son of God was placed in the womb of a virgin and his stepfather Joseph was a righteous man, not willing to make a public example of Mar. They were equally yoked—two people any of us could model our homes after.

*Who will you model yourself after? Kim is struggling—she is definitely in a place of sitting on the fence. Strong feelings for a young man who doesn't share her faith, and back home on Christmas vacation, remembering those cherished values and feeling the love of God in the atmosphere.*

At the conclusion of the service, Kim, Gloria, Zodie, along with most of the congregation headed downstairs for a fellowship dinner of roast chicken, peas and rice, snap beans and punch. The Christmas cake with the white buttercream frosting adorned with a red and green Santa and a nativity scene, and the joyous festive atmosphere filled Kim with such awe and thankfulness that she stood momentarily, eyes closed, hand clasped, and uttered a prayer of thanks. "Thank you Lord, for faith. I don't know what will happen to me and Eric but I thank you Lord for faith." And with that, Kim walked with a determination into the fellowship hall to sit with her family and the other worshippers.

# Love Yourself First
# (Then He can Love You)

Setting: The day before Christmas at the Smith household

Customers with last minute orders for the wellness products Gloria markets are calling off the hook. Doorbells and the telephone ringing competed with silver bells.

"Merry Christmas", "praise the Lord," "How pretty", "Thanks so much," "I know my (mama, auntie, homegirl, whoever) will like these, were the comments of the customers. Kim watched in amazement at how her mother multitasked and maintained such finesse under pressure: with the cooking, selling, baking, wrapping presents and keeping them hidden from peering eyes.

"Wow!" Kim thought. "How does mom do all this and never miss a beat?" As if reading her daughter's mind, Gloria said, "Baby girl, know this, When God allows something to be taken away from you, he makes something even greater out of the brokenness." She sat down beside her daughter, peering intently. "I know you miss your dad. I miss him too. Don't think that I don't miss hearing his voice, that throaty Barbadian accent when he announced "I'm home!" upon coming home in the evening. I may be walking spritely and doing all of these activities that make for success, but I have my needs. (Quietly) Sometimes in the middle of the night I think of him holding me. I think of the conversation we had about his dream to someday return to Babados and build that house by the sea, but then (a pathos caught in Gloria's throat and she paused, dabbing a tissue to her eyes.) Kim reached for her mother's hand. (Pause and continued) "All the faith in the world that you think you have doesn't prepare you when the hand of God intervenes and mixes up your plans.

"But ma," Kim protested, but Gloria said, "shh and continued. "I didn't know if I wanted to go on. I know what you are going to say, child. It wasn't God. It was the devil, but God had to sift it and allow the Devil to do it, so He knew what was going to happen. My faith was really challenged. My mind was so frozen and confused I was just going to die. I just wanted to go home and forget who I was. I looked at you precious girls and I wondered how I would take care of you. I felt like I needed a mother to take care of me. Who was going to take care of me? I tell you, I was ready to roll up in a cocoon and stay dormant." Kim listened in respectful silence and amazement as her mother unburdened herself. She never knew this side of Gloria that was ready to give up, to stop being a mother.

. . . "You know what? God woke me up from this state. It was a beautiful day, the daffodils were blooming, I hear a robin warbling and the Lord spoke to me ever so softly and said, "daughter, I have you covered. There is a hedge of protection around this family. No harm will come to you." I looked up to the heavens to ask, but why this?", but it was as if he supernaturally touched my lips and he told me I must move on. Later that night I read Jeremiah 29:11 "I know the things that I have for you, saith the Lord. Things to prosper you and not to harm you, to give you a future and a hope." (they recited in unison). "From that day on, I knew I had to move forward and not look back. I had to focus on the fact that the Lord is now my husband, and He gave me two wonderful girls to help nurture and He will fill in any gaps for protection that I cannot fill. Kim, Gloria said, still holding he daughters hand, I can't shield you from everything but this I do know, whatever experiences you go through, there will always be that hedge of protection around you." At that point, Kim felt her skin tingle as if it were a premonition of sorts.

**Proceed with caution as you follow that road map**

What are some signs that Kim needs to stop and read? Will proceed with caution be good enough, stop on red or just go ahead? Oftentimes the heart makes the final decision.

Gloria gave Kim several items to wrap for Zodie; some shea butter soaps and lotions; a heart shaped pendant with tiny diamonds surrounding the perimeter of it. Zodie's task was to create doilie place settings for each guest at the dinner table, come Christmas morning, and frost the spice cake, making the floral designs with a flick of the knife. Gloria, in the meantime, retreated to her room, discretely wrapping some last minute gifts and singing hymns of praise.

"It's now 9:30pm," Kim thought, "maybe I can just check my messages." Kim scrolled down the list of new messages, text messages: family, friends, two of the students from the Fisher of Men Club. "Sweet, but, not what I want to hear from right now," Kim thought, feeling a little frustrated and somewhat guilty for admitting that feeling to herself. She then rehashed that conversation that she and Gloria had earlier that evening. "Keep moving and going forward like mama,?" Kim thought. I want to have faith like that. Mama seems so happy and she works so hard, making others happy and being successful."

There's a saying in the Christian community that says Christians are like teabags. You don't know what they're made of until they're placed in boiling water. Then the flavor comes out. What flavor is inside of Kim?

Disappointed, Kim slowly scrolled through the received text messages. "Oh! wait a minute. How did I miss this one? I guess I missed the beep alert for my text message." Kim clicked the OK button to read Eric's message: "Hey sweet thing, you're my girl. Save me some sweet potato pie and fruitcake. Call you later. xoxo."

"Later? Tonight, maybe, I hope." Unlike the other messages that ended with "Merry Christmas, Eric's did not. Eric explained at one point that Christmas was an oppressive holiday, keeping the masses enslaved to materialism. Kim looked around to see if Gloria or Zodie were coming into the living room. "I'll turn up the volume of the radio," Kim thought. She didn't want either of them to inquire about who she was talking to. "There'll be time enough for them to find out" Kim thought. Taking a deep breath, Kim punched in Eric's cell number. After 6 rings it went to voice mail. "For God's sake, more power to the people" was the recorded tune from the Chi-Lites. (mild irritation) "You've called the right number but the man's on a mission. However if you leave your name, telephone number and a brief message, I will return your call, mission accomplished."

(Glancing around quickly) "Hey baby", Kim said, trying to sound as urbane and sophisticated as she thought Eric would like, "I'm hanging out with my folks, having fun. Sorry I didn't get your call. Enjoy your Christmas, oops! I forgot. You don't celebrate but enjoy your week off. Hope to speak to you soon. I love you."

# The Sister Circle of Friends

## Point #1 Home is Where the Heart Is

Christmas morning at the Smith residence:

The two nights before Christmas left Kim reeling with so many thoughts: Gloria's vulnerability, the closeness that she felt towards Zodie; the two of them reuniting as sisters; enjoying her friendship and not even being aware of her challenge, the black fruit cake, the pre-Christmas dinner, church, then of course, the hopeful spark at listening to Eric's voice message, and for the moment that was enough.

Anticipation—I could Hardly Wait

Funny, how Christmas brings out the kid in us: anticipating the new; something like when we find a new love, and could hardly wait to see them The new love is the new present, clothed in flesh.

## Dreams: A Harbinger of things to come

Kim glanced at the clock: 6AM. "I'll be the first one up, just like when I was a kid growing up; just let me wait another 15 minutes. The house was quiet; the dream was vivid, as vivid as 3-D. "love you, Kim. Let's try it one more time." "Wow! Eric's got some skills" Kim thought "This dream better not end yet." The atmosphere was a kaleidoscope of sights, sounds and colors. Even the smells: cinnamon and lavender fusing together to create a new floral note. Wow, what is this? Eric in a black tuxedo; Kim wearing an ecru lace dress. The background was in a large field with a few scattered flowers. It looked like a picture, yet the picture was 3-dimensional. How can I be in a picture and still be standing up at the same time,?" Kim thought. "Oh well, that's what dreams are made of." Then, the picture spins like a kaleidoscope, all the colors fusing into one—separate, yet together.

Next scene: sitting on a large white ivory pillow, large enough to hold them. Wait! we have on hardly any clothes! Eric, smooth chest; smooth as his voice; fawn colored skin; washboard abs; toned biceps, but not exaggerated like a 50 pound weight lifter. "Oh no! this is too fast" thought Kim. "Come on, Kim, you know you're my girl," Eric said, a note of desperation and demanding in his voice his eyes peering into her soul. "Oh no Eric, not now," Kim tried to protest, but the words just wouldn't come. He pressed her down on the gigantic pillow, chest to chest; his leg over her legs, and then, the picture spinned again like a kaleidoscope; music; the smell of bacon and eggs frying. "What now??" Spinning again, and then Kim woke up. "No surrender yet", Kim thought. "Gee, it's so bright, what time is it? 8:20!

The dream didn't seem that long; two hours later! "I wonder if that's what it would feel like if . . . oh no! I better not think thoughts like that," Kim said to herself, changing the subject mentally

"Merry Christmas big sis!" see what I got!" Zodie called out, a bit too loudly, intercepting Kim on her way to the bathroom. She held up the pendant with the tiny diamonds encrusted in the heart shaped perimeter. "Merry Christmas Zodie. It's pretty; very pretty. Now, can I get in here and wash up so I can open my gifts? Zodie stepped aside to let Kim into the bathroom. "OK" Wash up, apply Fashion Fair cosmetics. "I wonder what Eric's up to now?" That dream really makes me feel attached . . .

**Dreams can point you in the right direction. They can also be a harbinger of things to come; the beginning of one's demise with the wrong object of affections.**

"Merry Christmas, sleeping beauty" Gloria called out cheerily as Kim entered the livingroom. The lights were blinking on the Christmas tree. Zodie liked the blinking tree lights, day and night. Gloria served herself and her daughters a healthy serving of bacon and omelettes with Yuban coffee and the moccachino flavored liquid creamer was a blast. Temporarily, the desire for Eric subsided, as Kim flowed with the familiar routine of being back home with her family; Gloria, the loving hostess and mom always knew how to make things right.

Kim slowly got up from the table, stuffed, and walked over to the tree, sat down again to open her gifts. Zodie sat alongside her, expectantly, to see Kim's gifts and her reaction to them. "The gold charm bracelet with the 1/2" crucifix and the tiny sapphire stone; the cocktail ring, the poodle sweater with the mosaic of red and green; it was all touching and beautiful. Kim was very touched by the gifts and felt minimal about the gifts she gave Gloria; the mittens and the gold hoop earrings. Zodie received a pair of slipper socks with the toes and matching gloves. The sister circle of family and friends pulls together and gives life meaning.

**Enjoy the family connection.**

Will the foundation of family preserve Kim's integrity? or will the longing for Eric Baines pull her in a different direction?

What a pretty picture! Gloria, Kim and Zodie, sitting on the carpet on the livingroom floor, passing around and admiring each other's gifts. The dynamics of a family rooted and grounded in faith and committed to one another provides the groundwork for security.

*A Fine Piece of Chocolate*

Discussion Questions

1. How would it benefit Kim to talk about her budding relationship with Eric and her conflicting emotions?
2. What are some differences in the outcome of a relationship when women have a support group and when they don't?

In posing these questions among women in the faith community, those who had a support network expressed feeling confident as time went on that they can make it on their own. Think of cheerleaders rooting for their team. Those who did not have support, were more likely to feel depressed and anxious, and upon looking back, they really did not have a positive experience as they went about their healing alone.

# A Strong Family Brings Healing and Wholeness to One's Wellbeing

### Enjoy the Family Connection Before the Love Connection

"I love the poinsettia from Barbados especially," Gloria said graciously as Margaret handed her the box where the poinsettia can be viewed through clear cellophane. Margaret was Paul's oldest sister and was a matriarch of the extended family.

The family and neighbors held hands together, eyes closed, and gave thanks for the blessed incarnation of God's son; the gathering of family and friends; lives spared and, "O Father God, let us give thanks for Kim being home with us", young Vinny prayed, bringing Kim's wandering attention back to the fellowship meal. "Yes Lord!" the entire group said in unison, and, "Dear Lord, we give thanks for Gloria graciously opening her home to us and sharing her bounty with us, Andre prayed. He was greatful for Gloria's friendship after his wife left him and his daughter went astray, running the streets. Johnnie Walker Black became his friend, and Gloria would admonish him about drink being the wrong spirit. She would listen to him, pray with him, and gave him two plates of food when his funds ran low.

"Gee, Eric doesn't know what he's missing when he rejects the Christ of Christmas" Kim thought as the prayer ended. Everyone unclasped their hands and began passing around the Christmas bounty. The circle of family and friends around the table, coupled with the strains of Nat King Cole's "Merry Christmas" transformed Kim into a state of emotional completeness, independent of Eric Baines.

Hold on to those values when leaving
the safety of home

*(Setting: The end of the Christmas holiday. Gloria and Zodie accompanying Kim back to Newark Penn Station).*

Kim waved bye-bye to Zodie and Gloria as she boarded the Amtrak, heading back to Dayton.

"Write soon and write often", Gloria admonished, "between getting those A's and Bs."

"Thanks for the gift, Big Sis", Zodie waved, wearing the gloves Kim bought her.

"Stay pure and stay strong" was Gloria's second admonition. Kim winced slightly inwardly at that one. As she settled in her comfy seat near the window, viewing the naked, barren trees, limbs reaching toward the sky in the noonday son, she played back the memories of the Christmas holiday; the ride back home in the familiar Desius Weslande cab to the Sumpter houses; the juxtaposition of feeling familiar and different at the same time; reconnecting with Zodie and enjoying downtown Newark; finally hearing from Eric and talking at length with him, three days before New Year's. He apologized over not being able to meet up with her over the Christmas holiday, but, this is a New Year and he promised to "surely make up for the lost time he didn't get to spend with his boo." "I'll make it up to you, babe, I promise. My boys been pulling on me for the next CD and my folks went on vacation so I couldn't use the car, but anyway, next year is upon us, and I'll make it up to you babe, I promise.

"I don't know why he just didn't catch the Amtrak." Kim thought. After all, his dad is a successful attorney in downtown Pittsburgh". Just as quickly as the thought occurred to Kim, it disappeared again into her unconscious, and then she drifted off to sleep.

## Discussion Questions

1. How can a circle of friends and family be an emotional covering for a sista?

2. What can happen when that covering is not available.

Let me give you an example: One sista I interviewed described being embroiled in an emotionally abusive relationship with her son's daddy, who, in her words, held her hostage emotionally and almost convinced her that she could not live without him. Her sisters, who were Christians, encouraged her by repeatedly telling her that she *can* move on, get a job, and she didn't need him for anything. This sister, thankfully, received that truth in her spirit and did go on, get the job training that she needed, and landed a job in corporate America and is living comfortably on her pension. See what a little bit of faith can do.

## Know when he's not all that and move on

Setting: Arneatha is chilling with her friends, Bridgette and now Desiree, a new girl to the clique. "'neatha always has a crew around her," Kim observed, with a slight touch of envy.

"Hey little sis! so, what did the man in the red suit give you? (chuckle from the group). Kim felt a twinge of self-consciousness and mild irritation, as she was in no mood to be the brunt of Arneatha's jokes and didn't always know how to fend off Arneatha's jabs.

"Oh, a few accessories from my mom. It was nice. (then quickly added) "hey, where'd you go? what did you get?" A new coat and shoes, (voice trailed off) "so, what about that guy you been seeing? What's his name?

"Oh brother," Kim thought. "Now she's bothering me with these questions. How do I get out of this? (Desperately trying to sound nonchalant) Kim responded, "Yeah, we talked."

"Talked??" didn't you see him?

"Like I said, I was with my folks and he was in Pitts___ (interrupted)

"You didn't see him and he didn't get you nothin' before the break? (silence, as the group of friends turned towards Kim, waiting for her response. Kim (starting to lick her lips nervously and fighting the rising panic within her). "No well, it's OK. I had a nice break with my folks. No big deal.

"See these, little sis?" Arneatha said, holding up the red jewelry box with the oval shaped gold hoops and the bracelet with the jade and ruby stones. "Tyrone got me these". Kim wasn't sure if Arneatha was referring to the older (33 year old sugar daddy that she referenced from time to time, or someone on campus. At any rate, Kim was in no mood to be interrogated or to inquire about Arneatha's prospects.

"Well, it's a New Year now. It's all good," Kim said, her tone sounding a bit more tense than she wished to let on. After not too successfully fending off Arneatha's jabs, Kim retreated to the library to think—Does this budding relationship with Eric have a future? Is it just infatuation? should she give it more time? One thing she knew for sure, Kim definitely had feelings for the young swain; feelings that she never experienced for anyone else in her 18 years on this earth; and she would do whatever it takes to find the key to unlock the door to his heart.

### It Takes All Types of Men to Make the World Go 'Round

Dr. Lillian Glass, the "Body Language expert" profiled eleven types of toxic men. For the purpose of this discussion, it seems as if Kim found herself drawn to "The Selfish Me

Myself and I Narcissist. Kim, as a giving, trusting individual, is the perfect complement for one so self absorbed. However, the more giving the giver, the more the narcissist takes, until there's nothing left. Truly infatuation with a self-absorbed person is a dangerous thing. It's like sitting on a mouse trap. Anyway, back to Kim's story.

Kim found her favorite spot in the library to reflect and think of the past two weeks back with her folks, and the several phone conversations she had with Eric. Eric, visiting his folks and unable to make arrangements to spend time with her. "Maybe I assumed too much", Kim thought. Since Eric's family were people of means, it seemed as if he could make alternative plans if one car was out of commission. At the same time, Kim didn't want to seem too pushy, and brightened at the thought of them spending more time together once they were back on campus. In reflecting back on their conversations, Kim felt as if she held her own very well, and didn't let on too much on how much she wanted to see him. "Don't let them know too much, or there will be no surprise left," Gloria would admonish her from time to time. Kim smiled at the thought of Eric and her's conversation. Inadvertently, she found herself smiling at the strains of, "There Goes my Baby" playing softly on someone's ipod. That was the song she had programmed into her cellphone whenever Eric calls. *(Recapitulating back to a previous conversation they had)*

"Hi boo! Kim was surprised at her own forwardness in greeting Eric as she picked up the phone.

Eric—How did you know it was me?"

Kim—"I would expect to hear from my boo over the holiday."

Eric—(softly and smoothly) "hey, I like that. So, what are you up to?

Kim (attempting to sound lighthearted and nonchalant) "Been catching up with my folks out here in Newark, catching up with the sights and sounds in New York, put all the studying aside.

Eric—"I hear ya. I'm now with my folks in Pittsburgh for a few days before I return back to campus.

Kim—(a damper on her enthusiasm since Eric didn't mention anything more about driving one of the family cars to Newark, which he mentioned previously before she left campus to catch the Amtrak back to Penn Station. "oh" was all Kim managed to say.

Eric—"what's the matter boo?" Did I say something wrong?

Kim (quietly inhaling so as not to let it be known the disappointment she was feeling). "I just thought I'd see you for one day, that's all. We did mention before I left that you would be able to—

Eric (interrupting) "right, right. Well my dad's SUV minivan is in the shop right now, and him and my mom's gotta share the Prius . . .

(Kim lost track of Eric's explanation as she was really hoping they would get together for the holiday.)

Eric "Kim?"

Kim "yeah"? (Enthusiasm dampened)

Eric "I just asked you when you plan to be back on campus?

Kim "January 2rd, right before spring registration."

Eric "why do you sound so sad?"

Kim' (a bit of irritation rising within her at the realization that Eric could not seem to fathom her disappointment at the fact that as a couple, he did not have plans to see her over the Christmas and New Year's break."

Eric "disappointed?"

Kim (sarcastically) not *really* disappointed. I guess I assumed I was part of your holiday plans, that's all.

Eric—"well you were, (quickly) "I mean, are. If my dad gets he SUV repaired, maybe we could meet somewhere between Newark and Pittsburgh and hang out.

Kim—(thinking to herself) "don't count on it."

Eric "Kim, I love you."

Kim—"Thanks Eric."

Eric—"Thanks? I love you, Kim (sounding a bit more demanding)

Kim—"I love you too." (They both laughed).

Eric—See you back on campus, if we don't meet up this week and, I promise I will make it up to you.

Kim "OK".

Eric—I'll call you before New Year's. (Eric did three quick kisses over the phone.) Bye Sweetie."

# Be the Principal in the School of Your Heart

Life happens to all of us and we all learn something whether we plan to or not. When you first start out in life, you are a student. Life is the master that you learn from. Either you master life or life will master you.

*Point #1 The principal places priority on her goals and governs herself accordingly.*

Question: How will Kim master the challenge?

Setting: Spring semester is ready to begin. It's chilly in the Buckeye state. Kim spoke to Eric twice over the two week break. "Not enough time," she sighed. "Why does love hurt and feel so uncertain?" she thought. There goes the familiar ring of the cellphone. Kim jumps up as the ringtone, "There goes my baby" starts ringing. This is the ringtone for when that special someone calls.

Kim (breathlessly) "Eric?"

Eric (smooth as silk) "Sweetie, you knew it was me"?

Kim (trying to keep up with his smoothness and adjusting her tone to sound more casual) "well, when people are in tune or on the same vibe, like, you just know.

Eric "OK, OK, I gotcha. So, what are you up to?"

Kim "I just completed my schedule for spring semester. What are you doing?"

Eric—"finished playing a game of chess in the rec room. Gotta keep my game up to speed.

Kim (wondering what game he was really referring to, but didn't bother asking) "so, what's up otherwise?

Eric—"what're you up to lady?"

Kim I'm just getting my textbooks and be ready for next week and _____

Eric (cutting her off, something he often did). "Can I come by later, say, 6PM?

Kim "OK, that sounds great! (not bothering to check her appointment book first.


Setting—Kim straightens up her dorm room and looks at the menus from two different restaurants—one from Tex Mex and the other a Chinese, and imagined them seated on the couch, shoulder to shoulder, watching VH1 and immediately felt that oh, familiar feeling of warmth, cascading through her very being. Just then the phone rings, intruding on her thoughts.

Professor McAlister's student aide was calling to remind her of the appointment which was the last one for the day, at 6pm. Kim booked that appointment nearly a month ago and at the time, looked forward to meeting with the professor to discuss the biological and theological aspects of gender expression in children.

"Oh my!" (Kim thought, putting her hand to her mouth in consternation.) "What should I do? I knew I should have checked my appointment book before I said yes. Well, maybe I should call Eric back and postpone our date to later on next week" but quickly dismissed that idea. (Taking a deep breath).

"May I speak to Professor McAlister if she's available? (Brief silence, then the sound of Professor McAlister's strong voice over the phone.)

Kim—"Professor McAlister, I'm so sorry. An emergency came up at the last minute that I really have to take care of and I can't—

Professor McAlister (cutting her off) "Well, I have no further appointments until March. In the meantime, I really wanted to discuss with you how you plan to integrate theological concepts, which cannot be proven, into something as deeply personal as gender expression.

Kim—"well, I did want to speak with you, but can I come in next week? (pleadingly)

Professor McAlister (firmly) "I have no further appointments until March. In the meantime, your grade is a C-.

Kim (protesting) "but I included all the footnotes and studies supporting my viewpoint. (click) the phone went dead.

*Point #2 The principal takes responsibility for her actions*

Professor McAlister's reminder and terse message cast a pall on Kim's emotions, and at the same time anticipating her upcoming date with Eric.

Kim (pacing the floor back and forth). "Oh, why, I mean, I worked so hard on this report!, eyes brimming with tears. I wish Eric didn't call so early, dang! (stomping her foot). OK, I could've told him to meet me at Sheppard Hall and wait for me while I meet with Professor McAlister and defend my thesis, but Eric is so busy with so many things. Why! Oh why did this happen? Professor McAlister is a witch.

*Point #3 The principal does not get pulled in different directions, but does the pulling*

At 5:30, Kim's mood brightened and she put on the red, black and green boucle sweater and the Queen Nefertiti earrings that Gloria bought her for Christmas. "Well, it's alright," Kim reassured herself, putting the low grade in the back of her mind and thoughts of Eric in the forefront. At 5:55PM, the doorbell rings and automatically, Kim's heart leaps. Kim throws open the door and there's Eric, standing there in his J. Crew sweater and Stacy Adams shoes. "Hey boo", he says softly and Kim automatically closes her eyes and merges into Eric's arms. "Mmm" Eric murmurs to himself. There goes my baby. They hold on to each other for several minutes until Eric breaks the silence with, "you gonna let me in?" he laughs. Kim steps back and lets Eric in, and he takes her by the hand, guiding her to the couch. Kim has just upholstered the couch with a houndstooth throwcover, and is a little disappointed that Eric didn't take notice of the interior decorating.

Eric takes out a CD that he recorded with his group, the Sole-A-Dad trio and said, "let's listen to this one." Kim listened, leaning against Eric, her mind partly on the music, partly on the low grade from Professor McAlister and partly on her growing hunger pangs. "My man Earl gets real funky on that base" Eric said, bobbing his head to the rhythm.

Kim (to herself) "doesn't he think of anything else besides the Sole-A-Dad trio and politics?" Kim looked down at her hands as she was thinking.

Eric (noticing Kim's shifting of attention) "What's wrong, babe? You don't like this?"

Kim "no Eric, it's not that. How about some Chinese or Tex Mex?"

Eric—"enchiladas will be fine." Kim called the restaurant and placed a $20 order, receiving a free liter of soda as a thank you.

(The doorbell rings, Kim answers, and tips the delivery guy $2. Eric gets up and divvies up the order between the two of them. As he's divvying up the order, Kim feels suddenly very attached to him and reaches for his hand).

"Babe, I can't eat if you hold my right hand. Well, maybe I'll eat with my fork in my left hand and my baby on my right.

(They begin to embrace and lean down towards the couch. "Eric wait, not now, Kim murmured as Eric slid his slim tapered fingers down her blouse. She began to feel powerful, pulsating sensations that she never felt before with such intensity. It took everything within her to push Eric away and catch her breath).

"What's wrong"? Eric said, his facial expressions and voice a mixture of confusion, disappointment, and a touch of irritation.

Kim (feeling confused but determined to maintain a standard) "ahmm, it's just not the right time. I'm not ready yet. (yet??? Kim faintly heard the tiny scream of Gloria's voice in her conscience saying, "not ready yet?? You're not ready at all!!!" And just as faintly, Gloria's voice faded away.

Eric—"wow babe, you really never did anything like this before? You're really different from the other girls I know."

Kim—"what do you mean, all the other girls you know?"

Eric—"well, you start and then you stop, "It really is OK to go with your feelings, you know. Nothing wrong with that."

Conflicting emotions begin to interplay: the tension between what the Word is saying vs. what the world is saying; what you know is right vs. what you want to do right now. The student is seeking truth, but the principal is applying truth.

Eric (trying to convince Kim as she wavers on her posture). "OK babe". Next time I'll bring protection. The two of them held each other, looking into each other's eyes and Kim battling the rising tide of emotions threatening to take over her resolve.

Is Kim a principal yet? Or is she still a student? The good news is that the boundaries are still there but barely. There is still a recollection of lessons on what has been taught in the past and attempting to stand firmly in the present. One can only be considered a principal in the school of their heart when they have fully integrated their values into their current situation and are willing to walk away from any coveted situation that threatens their values.

# Knowing When Your Chocolate is the wrong flava and move on

(Setting—spring semester at Ohio State. Kim working on reports, her relationship with Eric, all in all a freshman transitioning from girlhood to womanhood)

"Professor Bahna's class is really a killer", Kim thought. There's so much politics involved in Urban Planning, it's amazing anything gets done." At that thought she smiled at Eric's pontification about the masses being held down by the ruling one percent. "That's my boo, Kim purred to herself, always fighting for a cause. (Sighing) "I sure wish he would spend more time for me instead of always trying to save the masses. Oh, but when he holds me and kisses me, it just feels as if everything will be alright." Just then, her phone vibrated and she automatically picked up. "Hey boo", came Eric's tenor voice over the phone. Whatcha doin this Saturday? (Kim's heart skipped a beat and she brightened at the thought of them being together, one on one.

"The Sole-A-Dad-Trio just finished cutting their CD, "The Acts of Man". Just want to know if my boo wants to come and show some love and support—(Kim felt some sinking disappointment at the thought of being one of many in a crowd, and after nearly two weeks of Eric being busy with his pet projects, she was hoping for something like a dinner date, but, alas, that wasn't to be.)?"

"Kim?" Eric asked, somewhat sharply. "You with me or what? I just asked you if you want to come on and show some support at Clayton Hall this Saturday?" (Not wanting to share her feelings as the timing would be wrong, Kim forced some happiness in her voice and brightly said, "sure Eric, I'll be there for you! What time is it?)

Eric (sounding less tense) "Eight PM."

Kim "I'll be there, 8PM sharp."

Eric—"Love you"

Kim "Love you too.

(Both simultaneously kissed each other over the phone)

Brightened by Eric's surprise phone call and their upcoming (support) date this coming weekend, Kim enthusiastically returned to the research for her Urban Planning report.

(Saturday evening: Kim is nervously preparing for meeting Eric and supporting him in the release of his debut album. She almost wished Arneatha was there to help her pull together an outfit that would really make a statement.) "Oh darn!" Kim said as she observed a zit coming out of her usually flawless skin. Quickly she went through her makeup bag to find some concealer. Finding none, she settled on pouring some alcohol on a cotton swab, dabbing the inflamed skin. She went through her closet to find something that showed sophistication and sexiness at the same time. The white, sleeveless I.N.C. dress with the diamond shaped design showed some possibilities. The dress from Dress Barn, no, it was too staid for an event like this. The sleeveless red ruffled blouse with the pencil skirt looked good for a career girl look, but, what can a sista put together to impress her man and show others that this is her man? The buzz of her cellphone indicating a text message distracted Kim for a moment. TRUST IN THE LORD WITH ALL THINE HEART AND LEAN NOT UNTO THINE OWN UNDERSTANDING. CB: XX2-XXX-XXXX

That was Gigi, Kim's prayer partner from the Fisher of Men Club. They met some months back and agreed to back one another up in the Lord in order to stay free from temptation on the freewheeling college campus. Kim started to text back a message, but she could not put together her thoughts, with all the excitement going on in her mind about the next few hours. Finally, she settled for some low rider skinny jeans, a camisole that showed some cleavage, and a Coldwater Creek jacket. Looking down at her feet which were crusty from a lack of TLC, Kim soaked them in the foot bath, and expertly scrubbed her heels and soles with the pumice stone, and clipped all of her toenails, leaving no uneven edges. Next, she put paper towels between each toe and slowly and expertly applied the clear nail polish, waited 20 minutes to dry, then applied rosebush red, waited for that to dry, then another coating of clear polish. Then she manicured her fingernails and applied some Sally Hansen nailsticks which were peel on designs, which mimicked time consuming nail art that some of the coeds paid $30 and $40 at the Lee Chee nail salon. Satisfied with her appearance, Kim looked one more time in the large, moon shaped mirror in her bedroom, smiled at herself, picked up her clutch bag with the gold chain shoulder strap, and exited her dorm room with the confidence of a pro.

# Keep Your Eyes Open and See the Signs

As Kim approached Clayton Hall, she felt her confidence wain somewhat when she saw the size of the crowd and some of the gangsta rappers sporting Varsity Jackets, Sean John Jackets, and some of their girls wearing K&C Leather Egyptian Varsity jackets and Ripcurl Ghetto Love Pants. They stood and nodded silently at the wannabes who loudly greeted them with "hey! what's up. Kim observed some of the same posturing as when she was back in Newark. Then there were groups of Asians, whites, and various curious onlookers who wanted to see and hear the Sole-A-Dad-trio for the first time. Kim had to admit she was impressed by the large following that Eric's group had. It seemed as if all of his practicing, recruiting and politicking paid off. The flyer he circulated around campus was very professional looking, Kim thought as she picked up one off of the ground. Momentarily she wished that she contributed to Eric's claim to fame, then her thoughts went back to trying to find him in the crowd. As she stood alone, scanning the faces in the crowd she felt a firm hand press their arm on her right shoulder. She jumped as it wasn't Eric's touch. Kim looked up into the eyes of David Tank, a young man in her English class who Kim felt liked her, but he always seemed awkward and a little goofy. Hi Kim. (He smiled down at her, kindly). At 6 foot 5, he towered over many and had an awkward gait. "If he was more confident and not so dorky, maybe I'd be interested in him", Kim thought to herself.

"Hi David." (Silence)

"Mind if I stand with you?"

"Well, ah, actually I was just looking for somebody." (David's face fell)

"But guess what, I'll see you in English class, ok?" Kim forced herself to smile at David. David brightened at that and started to ask Kim for her cell number, but she disappeared in the crowd to get away from him.

Kim stopped to look read a Langston Hughes poem on the wall, as she found poetry calmed her anxious nerves. As she was reading, Life Ain't No Crystal Stair and looked at the artist's rendition of the shadowy figures of the mother talking to her son, she felt as if someone was watching her. She turned slowly and there was Eric sporting a cream colored Stacey Adams suit and black shoes, a Giorgio Armani tie, and a gold baby stud in his left ear that Kim had not noticed before. "Eric!" Kim screamed and jumped to grab him. He smiled and held her back from grabbing him. "Can't get my girl's lipstick on my suit but babe, I will surely check you out after the show is over. He gave her a peck on the cheek as they walked through the crowd towards the side door where the celebrity acts go through. Several girls in the crowd screamed Eric's name and one of them ran up to him from the side, pulled him toward her and gave him an aggressive kiss on the cheek. Kim instantly felt rage rush through her, as she was now feeling a bit territorial. "Hey Simone", and he muttered something inaudible and disappeared into the corridor.

Kim found a seat in the auditorium and was feeling a wave of mixed emotions. Who really is Eric Baines. Where does he fit into my life? Was that girl or those other girls for that matter, just part of his fan club or something more? Arneatha did warn her about wannabes and groupies that follow around these musicians. The knot in the pit of her stomach just wouldn't go away. "I don't even feel like we're a couple now" Kim thought to herself. (The DJ announces various acts debuting at the event, reminiscent of America's Next top Model.)

"Finally, what everyone's been waiting for all night long (the DJ announced) Eric Baines and the Sole-A-Dad-Trio!!! The entire audience stood up in unison to applaud. Kim jumped up and down, clapping like when she was in church, moved by the Holy Ghost. Several girls hollered, "Eric! my baby! Ooh-ooh my baby!"

"Good evening, good evening" Eric smiled into the crowd with a mischievous twinkle in his eye. "How's everyone doin'?"

A cacophony of choruses from around the auditorium. "Great!" "Hanging in There" A lone voice shouted, "I love you, boo!" Kim looked around quickly but couldn't discern who it was in the dark. Then she remembered Arneatha's statement about the wannabes and comforted herself with that thought.

After some adlibbing and a few stabs at humor, Eric announced, "Let me, or rather let us, extending his hand toward the two members of the Sole-A-Dad-trio, entertain you tonight. The musicians in the back banged on the tambourines and the drummer worked up a frenzy. The songs had a nice fast tempo and the way the trios crooned there ooh ooh oohs sent a shiver down Kim's spine. Nothing but nothing could hold her together when Eric sang the solo for Usher's rendition of There Goes My Baby. She clasped her hands together and squeezed her eyes shut whispering ooh, ooh baby to herself, oblivious to everyone around her, especially when he said, "I'm dedicating this to my girl." Kim assumed this was her role. "Me and Eric. Eric and me." It's gonna be me and him. One on one", she thought to herself, hands clasped to her face, eyes closed and smiling.

At the end of the concert, Kim sat in her seat and waited for him in the auditorium, as he instructed her, not going to the back where all the wannabes and people asking silly questions, wanting interviews and signatures." Finally, after waiting for what seemed like an eternity, Eric entered from behind the curtain, wearing Benetton sunglasses across the top of his head. Smiling, he walked toward Kim and held both of her hands, lifting her to her feet. "Hey my little sweet thing, waiting so patiently for me, let's go." He led her out of the auditorium, (rather quickly) Kim thought, nevertheless happy to see him and be with him. They walked a distance from Clayton Hall and without a word, Eric kissed her hungrily. Kim squeezed him so tightly that if she held him any tighter he'd melt right into her and oh, how she would like that. They broke away from each other. Eric? How about the Ranch Diner? Eric looked horrified at forgetting this. He muttered something about having to collect the instruments and clean up the auditorium. Kim wailed, "But what do you mean? See, I got all dressed up for you, your my guy and after your debut, you don't even take me out like you had planned?" Suddenly summing up strength out of nowhere she said, "forget you, your not my boo! We don't go anywhere!"

"Wait a minute Kim! I'm sorry! No, wait, please, I can explain. I'll make it up to you the next time! I promise! I really, really promise!

(Setting: Kim in her dorm room, still brewing over the broken date and not answering her cell and text messages from Eric. It was tempting to pick up the calls, but, she wanted to give Eric a taste of his own medicine. Enough is enough already! How long is a girl supposed to wait on a guy to make time for her? After the fourth day, Kim picks up. She smiles as she thinks of how Eric never called or texted her so frequently. "Maybe there is something to playing hard to get that Arneatha told her about . . . that is, if you can keep on holding out long enough.) Finally she picks up and waits for Eric to speak.

(Silence) "Hello? Kim say something.

Kim—"I know it's you Eric."

Eric—"Baby, why are you acting like this towards me, like you don't understand?

Kim—(thinking to herself, "is he serious? Which of us is playing stupid? Nevertheless she did not utter her thoughts.)

Kim, answer me?

Kim—"Eric, I feel sometimes, no lots of times, that you're just playing games with my head and taking me for granted. Sometimes I call and text, and you don't return my messages. I feel like you just don't have the same feelings for me that I thought you did. I'm just tired of being set up and let down. I gotta get by myself and heal, you know?"

Eric (softly) "But I can heal you and you know, I'm sorry. I don't want to lose you and I really meant it when I said "I'll make it up to you. (Pause)

Kim (melting) really? (smiling)

Eric—"I've had time to think. Let's go to the Rodeo Diner this Friday evening. Are you game?"

Kim "You bet!"

# Falling Into the Hands of a Narcissist

The me, myself and I narcissist is a subtle game player. According to Dr. Lillian Glass, the narcissist loves himself. These men only know the words, "I, me, and my." Eric was self absorbed and loved talking about his goals. The narcissist rarely asks about what the person on the other end is doing. While Eric talked a lot and showed Kim affection from time to time, he had a tendency to be noncommunicative in terms of Kim not being able to get a hold of him and knowing his whereabouts. As is typical of a narcissist, they love being the center of attention and having attention showered on them. When Eric felt he might be losing Kim, for the time being he played the role of the remorseful suitor in order to win her back. How long will it last? Only time will tell.

Remember, there is always a way to escape—IF you take it.

(No temptation has seized you, but such as is common to man, but God has provided a way of escape . . . I Corinthians 10:13)

Such deja vu. Kim sitting across from Eric at the Rodeo Diner, similar to her first date four months earlier in Dayton. Four months already? Wow! time moves so quickly. This time, Kim agreed to a real Pina Colada, as Eric called it, with her dinner. "My baby is growing up" Eric said, smiling approvingly. The music in the background was a mixture of 60s, 70s, and 80s pop and R&B, similar to the sounds of WBGO in Kim's native Newark. (to herself Kim was thinking—"maybe we need these fights and makeups more often), but for now this was great. Then some slow jams came on; The Four Tops, Smokey Robinson, what Gloria liked to listen to at home. As if reading her, Eric leaned forward and whispered, "would you like to dance?" "Only with you Eric" Kim replied. They got up from the table for two and walked to the small space in the center of the floor reserved for dancing. Eric held her close, murmuring something that Kim could not quite hear, but nevertheless it felt good to be held so close that they felt as if they were one flesh.

All too soon, it seemed, it was time to return to campus. "Keep sweet, boo," Eric said, giving Kim one last soulful kiss before he walked off into the night, back to his dorm.

For the rest of the week, Kim was floating on air. Now she knew Eric confirmed his love for her, and for the time being she trusted him, but maybe too much.

Setting: Kim sitting in Eric's dorm room. "he's really neat for a guy" Kim thought to herself, looking around and seeing that every book was in place, shoes were stacked in the shoe rack, the CDS were in alphabetical order.

"What are you thinking, babe?" Eric asked as he placed his arm behind her head as she sat in the loveseat next to him.

"You like to keep things in order, really neat!"

"Yeah, I like my room neat, my women." (Eric leaned into Kim, covering her face with his kisses).

"Your women?" Kim asked, starting to pull away.

"My woman", Eric corrected himself emphatically, kissing Kim more passionately.

(Thinking to herself—Gee, maybe I should get up and get some water or something, just to change the tone of the evening.)

The television was a rerun of Keenan Ivory Wayans but neither of them were watching this now.

Suddenly, Kim felt the urgency of the passion building up in her, and realized that she really did not want to stop. Eric, sensing Kim's readiness, began unbuttoning the sleeveless print top she wore and buried his face in her cleavage. A low moan came from Kim's lips and she felt the wetness of her womanhood building up. Eric helped Kim get up off the couch, and help carry her flexible limp body into his bedroom a few yards away. Realizing the inevitable, Kim felt chilled and self conscious.

"What's the matter, babe?" Eric asked.

"I feel a little cold" Kim said, teeth chattering.

"It's okay, I'll warm you up" Eric replied.

Eric pulled off his dress shirt, and his undershirt revealed, smooth, firmly toned biceps. (just like in the dream) Kim thought to herself. He slid out of his trousers and boxers, and unfastened Kim's slacks and pulled down her panties at the same time.

"Oh God forgive me this one time I'll never do it again," Kim begged God silently. She reached down and felt his manhood and he was bare. "Ah uhm, do you use protection? I never did this before" she asked him.

"Oh I'll pull out I promise. I don't want to make no babies either."

Even though she was damp and awaiting his penetration, the pressure of his hardness pressing against her tight hymen became very painful and soon Kim was hollering out for Eric to "please stop! I beg you please!"

"It'll be over soon babe, relax. Just hold on to me tight." Just as he broke her hymen he pulled out, ejaculating warm semen on her thigh.

"At least he kept his promise not to get me pregnant" Kim thought.

(They lied in each others arms wordlessly, neither one wanting to break the silence of this sacred moment.

# Where is the love
## (that you promised me?)

Setting (Kim is in her room, calling Eric.)

"This is Eric B, master blaster of the Soledad Trio, the sound of revolution coming your way. If you reached this message, I am empowering the masses for change you can believe in. Please leave your name, time of your call, and a brief message after the beep."

Kim clicked off the message in frustration. It was the third time she attempted to reach him in two days. "How darn busy is my boo supposed to be?" she thought to herself. A creeping sense of unease began to well up inside of her innermost being, but she squashed it with other thoughts.

**Beware of rationalization**

"After all, we're both in college studying. I guess when you are a politician, musician, and a student all rolled into one, you don't own your time anymore."

Disappointed, Kim took a walk through Clayton Park, killing time until her next class in two hours.

(Springtime—renewal, rebirth. Being born again. Isn't that what Jesus talked about? The atmosphere, charged with expectations. Moms to be, some with toddlers in tow, strolling through Clayton Park; groups of teens, jostling around with friends. Couples, some with the ring of commitment on their fiancee's ring finger, others, without that obvious sign but still sporting commitment through their hand holding, slow walking pace, and frequent eye contact. Kim felt a twinge of envy several times upon viewing these couples.

"Why can't that be me and Er___ Suddenly, something caught her eye in the distance that made her rise from her sitting position. Kim placed her hand over her eyebrows to shade from the sun.

"That guy in the distance, walking with that girl, squeezing her shoulder like that's his boo, no, that isn't him, but it sure looks like him from the back." Kim thought to herself.

"Just walk up behind them and get a good look. After all, shouldn't you really want to know?" came the conflicting thought to Kim. On the other hand, "But what if it is really him? What would you do? What would you say to him? to her? What would you like to do to her?" "No, (more calmly as if to convince herself). "It's not him. There's other guys who wear that brand of a blue suede jacket and brown leather boots with the gold trim. These aren't one of a kind merchandise.

(Intrusive thought returns) "Yeah but statistically the height, weight, build, gait, is it all a coincidence?'"

"No!" Kim said out loud again to herself, to the intrusive thought coming from within, feeling self-conscious now when she realized that a lady pushing a stroller turned around and looked at her just a second too long. At that point, Kim walked in the opposite direction, wishing she had her ipod to play some music and wash away those intrusive thoughts.

## Discussion Questions

1) What do those intrusive thoughts and questions really mean?

2) Is love an all consuming passion?

3) What does it mean if you call him and he doesn't call back?

To quote Dr. Lillian Glass, "Trust your gut and never ignore the signs." Do you respond to that knot in your stomach that tells you that something is not right.

Kim, like so many young women on college campuses is thrilled with the young adult atmosphere but not exactly sure how to handle the menu. That's right. There is a menu of opportunities presented everyday, throughout the day on college campuses across America. The choices presented are all for better or for worse, and they all have consequences. Just like the voice which Kim heard from her innermost being, warning her that something is not right, women have to listen and be aware of the reality that the love and security they are seeking from a particular man is not there because he's just not available.

Setting: Back in the dorm room with Kim and Arneatha. Arneatha is probing, as usual, and Kim eventually breaking down and confessing that she and Eric had become intimate).

Kim is perusing through her sociology notes, ruefully glossing over Professor Bahna's comments on lack of depth and clarity. "Oh what the heck! I'm not gonna use this for the rest of my life anyway! Kim hissed with a sucking of her teeth."

Arneatha looked up from flipping the remote to different channels. "Whew! my little sis is on the warpath. Don't care about nothin' no more. What's a matter? Love got your nose open or closed or what?"

"I'm just saying! (Kim said defensively). I don't need this for my life. Let me just, you know, complete this project and move on with my expectations."

"Like what?" Arneatha said quietly, almost too quietly for her usually rambunctious personality. Kim stood frozen in a Kodak moment and stared at Arneatha without saying anything. Starting to feel her bottom lip tremble, she looked away quickly and began sorting the pile of clothing to be ironed, pretending to be looking for an outfit to match. (Again) "What up, Kim?

Kim realized that she could not ignore Arneatha's persistent probing, took a deep breath, quickly wiping her eyes and nose with her sleeve, turned and faced her.

"Okay, it's really okay," Kim responded with a false bravado, denying the pain the pain she was really feeling.

Arneatha—"Kim, we been roommates since September. Stop bs ing me. You were straight up, square, wanting to do the right thing and impress the professors, get to class on time, everyday, no matter what. Now it's like, who gives a whatever. It's like, all the time. What gives? (Silence, and then some more silence.)

Arneatha wasn't going to give up, not getting an answer. A part of Kim wanted to explode at Arneatha, telling her to back off. The problem was, Kim did not have the courage to say it. On the other hand, a part of her did want to share sister to sister what was going on in her life, but please, without the sarcastic jabs, thank you very much.

Kim—"Well, things get in a funk sometimes."

(Arneatha) cutting her off, rather impatiently. "Look, you're not the only girl on campus this happened to _____

Kim (quickly) you mean, with Eric or do you mean some other girl in general?

Arneatha (somewhat evasively) "It means whatever you want it to mean. (then quietly) "He was the first, wasn't he?" (Kim turned away without answering, stifling her sobs.)

Arneatha gazed at Kim's back, waiting in respectful silence before continuing.

"Yeah, you had a playa alright."

Kim froze, as if her worse fears were now being confirmed.

Arneatha (somewhat backtracking) "Look, he's your boo; just check him out. See who he hangs out with. Friend him on facebook; follow him on Twitter. Tweet to your sweet. Oh come on, Kim, get real. Get with the game. Have a game plan, OK?"

Kim wondered how much Arneatha really knew about Eric in fact. Being so close to finding out the reality was frankly, quite scary and a bit too overwhelming to ask. (Her head spinning, and wanting to keep her dignity and composure, managed a weak smile.) Thanks 'neatha. I will do my homework and look up his profile.

> He's a player, he'll get next to you
> He's a player, he'll know what to do
> He'll shoot you down,
> right down to the ground (2X)

(words from He's a Player, by First Choice)

## There is more than one way to be armed and extremely dangerous

Dangerous Dan is every decent woman's nemesis in First Choice's R&B hits. He catches unsuspecting women with their guard down, slides between their legs and keeps it moving. Raw but real. Women, have an arsenal of weapons for a counteroffensive when you meet this type of man ladies. Choose your weapons wisely. The wrong arsenal may become your undoing. Now, back to Kim.

Kim was reeling from that sista to sista talk regarding the insinuated revelation that Eric was a playa on campus. While Arneatha did not come out and say it directly, there was enough insinuation in her tone that stripped away any naivete that remained with Kim that Eric was simply building both his political and musical career. Still, she found herself clinging to one last thread of hope that she was his only one, or the main one at least and, if there was anyone else, they were just a passing fancy.

*Point—Do the detective work; Just make sure it's legal.*

Setting: Kim becomes obsessed about Eric's whereabouts. The charming, fine piece of smooth, caramel chocolate seems more and more busy these days, and at times even more abrupt and hostile when Kim inquires about his whereabouts.

"Kim, baby, stop comin' on like you own me or something.
"But"
"Like I said, I got sidetracked doing this soundtrack. I didn't mean tostand you up as you said. It was an accident, my bad_____

Arneatha's voice "You need to do some detective work on your man, that's all I got to say."

And detective work she did. She started by looking up Eric's profile on his facebook page. It seemed as if he had a lot of friends and fans. Dubbed as the fine piece of chocolate, smooth as silk lover. Kim stopped cold. Lover? whose lover and how recent is this?

## Obsession Leads to Disaster

Eric, sitting, always in the middle, with his friends. Beer in one hand and, who is that sista with the weave and the long painted eyelashes? She looked vaguely familiar, but Kim couldn't put a finger on the time and place where she might have seen her. Feeling a knot in the pit of her stomach and a lump as hard as a rock in her throat, threatening to cut off her breathing, like a woman obsessed, Kim pored through every comment on his face book page to find everything and anything she needed to know about him. Not wanting to know, yet wanting to know at the same time, Kim perused though his wall; comments people left. It seemed as if more than one young lady had more than a passing fancy for him.

Next scene—Kim getting more and more obsessed with finding out all that she can about Eric, to the point where she now rationalizes missing days of classes as she "researches" Eric's life, high school days, college applications; she gets a job in the college office as an intern, but spends time looking up Eric's confidential information.

"Oh well," Kim thought to herself; I can make up these classes over the summer. She received a letter warning her about being placed on academic probation for the incomplete in the fall term that will turn into an "F" if she doesn't complete the requirements by June. The essentials of general chemistry class, missing labs—academic probation. Red alert icon in her email. "Please see the freshman advisor to discuss these concerns. Failure to correct these academic issues can place your scholarship in jeopardy. Remember, we are here for you."

The friendly, pleading tone with its warning consequences came across loud and clear.

"I'll deal with this later," Kim thought to herself, as she went back to do her "research" on Eric.

She read and reread his facebook contacts; she stopped several times to view closely the two ladies who were friends" but more than just friends. How she wanted to meet them and scream that Eric was hers, first, or that Eric was her first, but what would that accomplish? What sort of girls did he really like? The ultimate pain was realizing that she was no where in his world on facebook. Why didn't he ask her to friend him, have a picture of the two of them on his wall, for all the world to see?

# New chapter: Time for Payback

Setting Kim leaving the college advisor's office, dejected after being informed that she wold have to make up two classes plus a lab, putting her scholarship in danger of being revoked.

Mrs. Tiemann (advisor) "Kim, Ms. Smith, I know this isn't you. These grades don't reflect the student who entered OSU with a 3.9 GPA. What happened?

Kim (biting her bottom lip nervously.) mumbled something about "I just fell behind. That's all." Mrs. Tiemann started to ask something, but thought better of it. she got up, announced, "well then I shared your options with you and I wish you a good summer and a better semester next fall.

What's there to live for?" Kim thought to herself. "Eric, he'll pay. I swear."

Time passed quickly and Kim was in such deep thought as she returned to her dorm room, fantasizing revenge, that she hadn't heard when Arneatha returned. Kim jumped out of her love obsessed revelry at the sound of Arneatha's voice.

"You sure you okay, Kim?" (then pausing) don't tell me you got knocked up by loverboy."

"No!" Kim said rather crossly."
"Well, it don't seem like you two are tight at all."
"'neatha, just leave it, OK? Things are workin' out the way they're supposed to. Isn't that what you say?" Kim said with a nervous laugh.

(Arneatha) "yeah, but how are you handling it?"

Kim (slapping her hands to sides for emphasis. "Cool, everything's cool," she responded.

Arneatha—"yeah, well, just don't cross any bridges or jump over any bridges."

Kim (thinking to herself) "what does she mean by that? I know I'm not crazy.

(Setting—Kim perusing through Eric's confidential college file.)

Whoa! Caught cheating on his SATs! Since his dad, Eric Baines Sr. is a high profile attorney in the Pittsburgh area, it seemed as if his dad got this expunged from his high school record. The Pittsburgh Courier ran a small article about a cheating scam that broke out among a group of students at the boarding school where Eric Jr. attended. The school officials still weren't sure how they gained access to the questions for the SAT, but a school official commented that "in this digital age, the best and the brightest have the know how to access anything." At any rate, the charge was reduced to a misdemeanor, and Eric had to simply do 35 hours of community service, coaching basketball at a local middle school, nevertheless. Upon further perusal, Eric was on academic probation twice during his freshman year, even when pontificating that he had all things under control, and "a man, if he is to be successful and gain the confidence of the masses has to have focus and excel in all that he does." Excel? He was falling down even while excelling!

Upon hearing approaching footsteps Kim quickly closed the file cabinet and went back to alphabetizing the course offerings for the upcoming fall semester.

"Now I have enough ammunition to shoot down the politician," Kim wickedly thought to herself.

**Beware of revenge: It is like spitting in the wind.**

"Might as well get the job done, since, after all, I have to go to summer school," Kim rationalized to herself.

Loading her laptop in the library, sitting in the quiet familiar place where she and Eric once shared soft, quiet conversations and soulful kisses, only fueled Kim's passion to put him on blast. Writing on Eric's facebook wall she blasted, "POWER TO THE PEOPLE?? REALLY!! A KNOW NOTHING SCAM ARTIST. THAT'S WHO YOU ARE." SIGNED, FROM THE ONE WHO REALLY KNOWS YOU.

Satisfied over the e-blast that she was sure that many would read, Kim went back to studying the humanities material and complete the overdue assignments before summer school began.

**God sends out warnings before a fall.**

"Let him who thinks he stands take heed, lest he fall."
(I Corinthians 10:12)

(A text message from Gloria: "Hi baby. The Lord just laid you on my heart. Is everything OK? Call me. I'm in your corner, you know."

Upon reading this, Kim felt unwilling tears well up in her eyes that she tried to blink back. "Oh mama, if only you knew. I know you'd be sad, but I can't tell you now" Kim said softly to herself. She glanced over at the small pocket Bible, lying unread since—when? Before Easter. It seemed like eons ago when Kim entered OSU, beaming with anticipation over college life and promising her mom, sister, and the youth group at First Corinthian Baptist Church that she would stay in the Word while pursuing her studies. It seemed like eons ago when she was an active member in the Fisher of Men's Club, enjoying the fellowship and the inspirational services. All these things so-long-ago.

(Setting—Kim walking through campus, books in her backpack which was rather light these days, running into Melanie from the Fisher of Men's Club.)

Melanie had a vibrant personality and a confident persona that appealed to Kim.

"Well, where have you been hiding at?" Melanie asked.
"Oh hi Melly, what's up? Don't mean to be missing in action. How are ___ (cutting her off)
"Yeah, Deena and James, they said they haven't seen you either in sociology. Everything OK? You know, we have to bear one another's burdens.
(Kim, faking a laugh and a smile that she didn't really feel). "Everything's OK, really! Hey, I gotta run to the library and complete this overdue project. Let's keep in touch, OK?"
At that, Melanie took out her cell and asked Kim for her number. Kim, (swallowing a slight rise of impatience, stated: XX3—XXX-XXXX). "See ya."

Arriving at the library, Kim took out the make-up exam to complete. She promised Professor Moffat to have it all completed and e-mailed by May 1st. (May Day, as it is known on a campus. Halfway through the project, Kim stopped and googled, Sole-A-Dad Trio. "Wow! 1,073 hits and it's in one of the top 10 in search engine rankings!" Feeling the uncontrollable obsession, Kim pored over every piece of online information.: their scheduled tours over the summer. "No time for me?" Kim thought with a tearful pathos, now being replaced by a burning resentment.

Suddenly, her eye caught an announcement for a benefit concert the Sole-A-Dad Trio was hosting at Sheppard Hall on Saturday, May 12th, 8pm.

*Bring two cans of non-perishables and new or gently used clothing for the victims of natural disasters throughout the midwest and Atlantic regions. $10 donation, $5 if you donate two non perishables and a piece of new or gently used clothing.* Kim saved this event in her cellphone calendar, although how can she forget?

**Beware! Time Wasters Can be Costly.**

Wow! You could find out anything you want to on the 'net, Kim thought eagerly as she perused through blogs on, "Successful Revenge Tactics when your man is cheating." One blogger wrote how she scouted out her ex and sitting in a rented van a safe distance away, observed a job of workers replacing old vinyl siding with new, powder blue siding. She got red spray paint from Ace Hardware and dressed as a ninja, drove over one night and saw that he was out, and spray painted a blizzard of crimson red paint all over one side of his house.

Revenge is sweet.
Signed,

Sweet Revenge.


Some antics were funnier than others. Kim instinctively avoided those blogs involving harassing or threatening an ex lovers kid. "Too evil," she thought.

She finally settled on two pieces:

The anonymous facebook and email assaults, and flatten the tire of the band's rented jeep.

"Keep him out of commission for a while," Kim reasoned.

Other revenge tactics included flooding his email with spam—all anonymous of course. "Anything to keep him from reaching his goals." she thought. The problem was, however, it never occurred to Kim that she was losing out on her goals.


**Beware of the Way Things Might Appear**

Over dinner, alone in the cafeteria, Kim felt the vibration of a text message. Who?? Eric?? what does he want? It's been well over a month, really, more like half a semester it seems since they were together at all. Fighting the anticipation and momentarily forgetting the revenge plan, Kim text back "What up?

"Meet me at Starbucks on West Lane Avenue."

Kim wondered why Eric, after this prolonged absence from her life would want to meet with her, just like in the old days. Though not much of a coffee drinker, Eric liked the atmosphere which he described as "great for networking."

Returning to her dorm room, Kim dressed carefully for the occasion, adding several coats of jade green mascara to her eyelashes, to make them look long and colorful, just like the competition. Next, she applied apricot blush to the apples of her cheeks. The long tweed sweater coat matched her willowy frame. The coral creme lipstick brought attention to her lips in a dramatic way. Oh, one more thing: a spritz of Halle Berry's Pure Orchid behind both ears, and then here, there and everywhere was the final accentuation.

For a moment Kim paused and asked herself, "why?" why get all dolled up for a guy who played on her innocence and for all practical purposes it is over?

But then came the answer: Look your best no matter what. Who knows? He may desire the fire once again and maybe, just maybe, I won't have to carry out the plot.

Kim walked along West Lane Avenue until Starbuck's came in sight. She slowed down, her heart pounding. What would she say to Eric? Why would he want to meet with her? After a brief hesitation, she walked in, glanced around the crowded Starbuck's. (It sure seemed to be the place to network.) Then she spotted Eric in the back right corner wearing the blue and white striped dress shirt and navy trousers that he wore on their first dinner date at her dorm room when he brought by the General Tso's chicken, laying out the plastic cutlery so expertly, just six months earlier. At that moment, Kim felt a strong wave of nostalgia hit her. She paused, regrouped emotionally, then strode purposefully toward the back table.

"Hi" Kim ventured shyly.

"Hi," Eric responded.

Several minutes of silence then Eric offered, "What would you like? (scanning the menu Kim decided on a mocha frappucino. Eric settled on a tall apricot tea, hot. "mild and flavorings to the right of you, the barista offered, after they placed their orders.

Eric—"I know I've been busy with gigs and what not, but let me tell you, I'm not trying to hurt you babe."

Kim—(somewhat relaxed) "Well, Eric, sometimes it seems as if you don't care anymore. I mean, you were my first and everything.)

Eric—"I know but giving it up is part of growing up. The good ole days that were portayed on Leave it to Beaver just don't exist. Hookups, if you are lucky, will be long term, much of it will be short term. No big deal."

Kim—"no big deal!!" Kim shrieked, her eyes flashing angrily, oblivious to the customers turning around at nearby tables.

Eric (facial expression like a smirk, a bit nervous as he did not like to call negative attention to himself.) nevertheless continued, "Kim, you weren't the only one." (Even though she was about finding out about Eric from the online postings on his facebook page, the revelation from Eric's lips was a bit too overwhelming."

Kim (in massive hysteria, totally oblivious to the Starbuck's crowd, shrieked "Even when I thought it was just you and I it really wasn't?? You'll pay for this!!" and with that she grabbed her coat, keys and purse, leaving the frappucino untouched.

("Straight from the horse's mouth" she could hear Gloria's voice in her head.

Now, it's time for revenge, Kim hissed to herself, totally forgetting about the time honored principles she was raised with, and her reason for attending OSU.

(Meanwhile, back at the dorm room, some days later)

Arneatha—(noticing the increasingly brooding attitude of Kim, had her sister circle, as she called her clique of friends, come by and watch some Tyler Perry dvds;)
"What up, Kim?"

"Oh, nothing."

"Been caught up with yourself these days. Got that brother on lock down or something?"

"I'd rather not talk about it, 'neatha."

"Well, we all got s—to deal with. Why not let it out?"

"Cause, I rather not talk about it. Plus, there's nothing to talk about" Kim said rather tersely.

Arneatha's friends turned to her, awaiting her response.

"You got something going on. I see you leave in the morning without your books, you come back late. No studying. A couple of those girls, I forgot who, knocked on the door the other day, saying they didn't see you in class and thought maybe you were sick and didn't contact anybody."

"Well, I'm not sick. Just so much to do."

"Did he put on a condom?" Bridgette piped up. (always willing to be Arneatha's sidekick).

"What? oh get outta here. It wasn't like that!" Kim felt her face flush and couldn't hide it.

"You still a virgin?" came another voice from the group.

Unwilling to admit what appeared to be obvious to all, Kim blabbered incoherently. "No! it's not that! Why are you askin' me all these questions. It's not—what is it to any of you anyway!!

(Kim fled to the kitchen, listening to their conversation in low tones.)

"She ain't been the only girl to get played," "It's life. Time to woman up and face life." "Just leave her. She'll get over it."

Arneatha walked in the kitchen quietly. "Hope you used protection," then walked out.

After a while Kim came out quietly and sat at the periphery of the group, watching Madea and laughing a laugh she just didn't feel.

*Point—Executing revenge is not always sweet*

Kim took some smug, bittersweet satisfaction posting inflammatory material on what a liar, cheat, and lousy lover Eric was, on facebook and on Twitter. Calling the politician a fake student with poor credentials gave her some really smug satisfaction. The anonymous postings were great and, knowing how Eric took pride in his reputation brought smiles of delight at the thought of seeing him squirm. Looking forward to May 12th, to slash the tires of the Sole-A-Dad Trio's van—well, if not all four tires, at least let the air out of one. Then the white spray paint to spray Fake Politico on the side of the van.

"That will make him really lose face with his people," Kim reasoned.

Finally the night of the Sole-A-Dad Trio's benefit concert arrived. Kim donned a disguise of oversized sunglasses, a plaid jockey cap, a black leotard and Skecher's sneakers. Not wanting to attract attention by anyone she knew, she packed the disguise in her backpack and wore her usual low rider jeans and oversized jacket, and left her dorm room around 7:45pm to avoid the crowd along West Lane Avenue.

Not sure if the ensuing heart palpitations were fear, Kim willed herself to move forward with the plan, "not taking the coward's way out", she reasoned. Watching at a safe distance, when it got dark enough not to be detected, Kim looked around, seeing nobody, she eased out of her jeans, slipped on her sunglasses and waited until an opportune time to slash the front tire. It would be harder to drive a van with the front tire flat than the back, she thought. Would there be time to spray paint "FAKE POLITICO" on one or both sides of the van? Kim estimated that the number of seconds to pull off this stunt might take longer than expected, especially since she was a novice and it was her first time doing this.

But I gotta do this, she hissed to herself. It wouldn't be worth the risk failing her courses and then not pulling this one off.

The problem was there were so many people milling around; entering, exiting, couples looking somewhere for privacy. Finally, it looked as if the crowd had settled in.

"Time to make the move, girl," Kim willed to herself, heart palpitating; doing her best to avoid the glare of the floodlight near Northwood Park. Under the cover of darkness she crept forward, looking around. Kind of hard to see at night with those sunglasses. "Maybe I should take them off," she thought to herself. Holding the can of spray paint, wrapped in a scarf she whispered, "better late than not at all."

Quickly, without looking around to see if anyone was around, Kim sprinted to the right front wheel, palms sweating, fumbling with the pocket knife; made several unsuccessful stabs at the rubber tire, not really sure if she made a sufficient puncture wound to disable the tire. Then, armed with boldness, she jumped back a few yards and clumsily holding the spray can managed to squirt FAK before she heard a voice yell, "stop her! what's she doing!!

In a panic, Kim took off in an adrenaline rush, not anticipating being spotted or even considered the possibility of being caught. Running, not sure of which direction she was running in, and then realizing in a panic that she left her jeans and jacket with her ID behind the big oak tree where she planned to run back, change out of her outfit in 10 seconds flat, and keep it moving.

"Oh great! what can I do now? If they find my clothes, my ID. Oh God! why is this happening to me?? God!! why!"

Finally, after much crisscrossing and zigzagging among W. Lane Avenue and North High street, and being spooked by the bright lights, thinking they were, (or getting confused with) police cars passing), Kim was exhausted and starting to feel chilled from the night air and perspiration that evaporated on her body. She sat on a bench at a bus stand, feeling sleepy and hyper alert at the same time, and hugging herself against the cold . . .

After awhile she got up and continued walking, eventually seeing her dormitory building in the far distance, and breathed a sigh of relief. "Home sweet home she thought, but, how do I get in without my key? and my ID? and I'm dressed like this? Oh rats!

Kim quickly concocted a story about visiting a friend, and thanked the matron profusely, agreeing to be more careful with her belongings the next time.

Point—*Sin can't always cover its tracks*

"Maybe I better pay more attention to my studies after all," Kim thought to herself rationally for the first time in a long time.

Later on that week, the OSU observer came out, nothing unusual but on the inside of the front page, and article, titled, Vandalism Mars Successful Fundraiser.

The Sole-A-Dad Trio, a neo-soul group held a fundraiser on Saturday for the victims of natural disasters in the Midwest and North Atlantic area. This otherwise successful event was marred by an act of vandalism; attempted slashing of a front right tire and spray paint on the left side of the vehicle. While no suspects have been apprehended, campus police are looking into the possibility of a disgruntled female suitor, possibly of the band leader.

Upon reading this, Kim's hands felt clammy, and she felt a foreboding of something inevitable about to happen. Later on that week, a sealed letter with the word, CONFIDENTIAL was handed to Kim by the matron. Trembling, Kim sliced open the letter, from the dean of academic discipline at 9AM, May 16th.

*The lord is my shepherd (guide me Lord)*
*I shall not want. (I want you more, Lord)*
*He maketh me to lie down in green pastures,*
*(Not on a jail cell floor, Lord)*
*He leadeth me beside the still waters,*
*(still waters run deep, and I'm drowning, Lord!)*
*He restoreth my soul.*

Trembling, Kim arrived at the dean of discipline at 8:58AM, holding her folded hands together that would not stop trembling. After a 10 minute wait, a stern faced Dean

Nguyen opened her office door and called her in, crisp tone. "Kim Smith!"

"These items were found 10 yards from the scene of where the vandalism took place. Do you know how they got there? There were her jacket, jeans, small leather pouch with her campus ID.

"No," she gulped.

"Well, cameras are installed all over the campus, and there was a picture taken of this alleged incident.

Kim broke out in a sweat and felt the color drain from her face. As the dean played back the grainy footage for Kim to view, Kim couldn't look at it. She looked past it; daydreaming of being some place, any place but here. Judgement day was now!

"Vandalism," dean Nguyen continued, "is very serious and is grounds for dismissal from Ohio State University. Furthermore, you are failing two subjects and have not made up the missing work from your philosophy class"___The mediator who was assigned as Kim's advocate interjected that "the make-up work is in the process of being submitted by Ms. Smith, and she will make up any outstanding work over the summer."

Dean Nguyen interrupted, "the course completion for the fall incomplete was not submitted and therefore the grade has been changed to an F. Any Fs on a transcript of a scholarship student places the student in danger of having the scholarship revoked." Kim felt a rush of tears and furiously wiped her eyes with her sleeve. Dean Nguyen continued, "According to the requirements of her scholarship, Kim has to maintain a GPA of at least 2.0, the minimum anywhere. Her GPA is now 1.75.

"Extend the probation," mediator Jackson pleaded. While Dean Nguyen's tone softened somewhat, her resolve was firm. "We have standards here at OSU and if we turn a blind eye and a deaf ear to poor performance and vandalism, the university standards will decline."

Kim felt absolutely surreal about this dream, her reality, about being in OSU and now having to leave in disgrace over what? A guy? A good for nothing who really wasn't hers to begin with?

## Discussion Questions

1. What signs of danger could Kim have avoided?

2. How did Arneatha's character change over the course of the school year?

3. We may choose our actions but not our consequences. What does that mean?

Over the next four weeks Kim made plans to pack and return to Newark. While she couldn't bear to open up and tell Gloria the ugly truth, Gloria, with her depth of perception, knew.

"I need to come back home mama," Kim said tearfully over the phone. I need to be home with you and Zodie."

"I know, baby. You're always welcome. This will always be your home."

On the last day of spring semester, the week before summer school would have started for her, Kim carefully packed both of her suitcases; sunglasses concealing her red rimmed eyes. She paused, then gave Arneatha a big bear hug. For a second, it looked as if there was a tear in Arneatha's eyes. "Take care, little sis, you'll be OK." There was the honk of the cabbie waiting impatiently as Kim hurriedly dragged her two suitcases to the waiting cab, paused, and took one last look back at the dorm building where birthed and then shattered. "I have a new purpose from all of this," Kim encouraged herself, with a new found maturity beginning to bloom in her, as the cab headed to the Amtrak station for the train back east to Newark, New Jersey.

# Redemption after Fallout

<u>Point—The journey back to redemption is painful but necessary</u>

"It really is all about you, Jesus," Kim said, clasping her hands up close against her chest, eyes closed; a small trickle of tears rolling down her cheeks. Eric Baines wasn't worthy of her cherry, her gift to that one special man that she hoped to spend her life with. He was nothing but empty words, a hollow politician making promises he didn't keep. Like a smart, former constituent who votes with her feet, Kim slowly, made her way up to the aisle to rededicate her life, broken heart, shattered dreams but a wiser soul.

I'm coming back to the heart of worship
And it's all about You
It's all about You, Jesus

Amidst the weeping at the altar, Pastor Phillips, the visiting guest pastor, addressed the youth, describing his rugged life in rural Jamaica as a youngster: hungry, bright, inquisitive, was a drug runner who almost lost his life in gang warfare. The taste of the fast life was so attractive that he bypassed and lost opportunities that would have gotten him on the road to recovery and redemption earlier.

"God gave me this limp as a permanent reminder of my sin when I was running for the devil. I'm not ashamed today. Young people you don't have to run with the burden of sin for 30 years the way I did. Some of you just started on the wrong path of sin's broad way. It's not too late! Come back young people. God is a God of the second chance. Young lady, hold your head up high. Don't be ashamed. Jesus gave the woman at the well back her dignity. He will do the same for you."

At that point, Kim crumbled in a heap at the altar, sobbing a mixture of sorrow, regret, and relief all at once. She felt the presence of the Lord through the hand of Sister Marguerite, helping her to her feet. "It's a new beginning my sister, ministry is being birthed in you. Let the Lord turn your sorrow into joy."

## Point#2 Put things into perspective

Kim walked back to her seat and gave thought to her first year of college. Now, it's time to put things into perspective.

Putting things into their perspective. Perspective is the lens that enables you to see things the way they really are and not through rose colored glasses. How many times, ladies, have you viewed your man from the perspective of how he makes you feel, (on a good day). Let's face it ladies, the couples you see hugging up on Broadway going to the theater may not be that way behind closed doors. Seeing one's experiences as the birthing of ministry provides healing to the listener as well as the speaker. Kim knew she had a new beginning awaiting her from that moment on, and her future was just beginning.

<u>Setting:</u> Covenant Keepers for college age girls and women ages 16-26, at Kim's home church, First Corinthian Baptist Church. The sister in charge of the discussion presented some analogies and handed out scenarios on what what would you do if . . . (description of scenario. They broke up into small groups where they discussed how they would handle certain ethical and moral dilemmas.

"I knew right from wrong," Kim thought to herself, "and I always thought I would do the right thing, learn a lot of facts, enjoy new campus friends, get to know some nice Christian guy, and marry a guy just like my dad. What happened?"

The sister in charge of the discussion presented some analogies and handed out scenarios on what would you do if you found yourself in particular situations. One group discussed the options of a Christian girl facing a very early pregnancy during her first year of college. The advice she was getting was: "it's not fully formed; your guy may not stick around; they usually don't. You can get married after college. She has the pressure of being the very first one in her family ever to attend college. Can she make an exception to God's perfect moral law just this once?" Kim felt a pang at the statement, "just this once." The reminder of Eric's persuasive, "just this once," followed by the black hole of deceit and disappointment. "But it's over,"

Kim reminded herself. "I am healed, now I must heal others." As the members of the group swapped comments about the sista in the pregnancy dilemma, making statements such as: "she shoulda known better", "my momma had me before she was married", "it's a life, she could always go back to college," Kim suddenly found herself standing up without realizing it. She gulped and began to address the crowd, saying: "I know what it is to know better, but something seems so right that I walked right into it. Once I walked into it, I couldn't back out. I felt different. I knew I was changed and I wasn't the same. The relationship changed. I found out I wasn't the only one. I wanted to kill him and hurt him for hurting me. I went on cyberspace to ruin him and wreck him, and I almost ruined myself. (Pause) Sometimes getting even and exacting revenge seems so sweet. But, a wise person once said that revenge is like spitting in the wind. It comes back to you. I felt like pounding my head into a rock, but you know, the only one left bleeding would be me."

(The room was completely silent as the young women sat listening to Kim with rapt attention.) Starting to feel self-conscious at the realization that she was the focal point, Kim took a deep breath and then continued. "I put my faith on the back burner while I pursued a relationship that ignited my passion for lust and not for God. Even my studies took a back seat. School didn't matter. God didn't matter. Sometimes it seemed as if life didn't matter. When I saw this guy wasn't one with me as I was with him, it was like, my life was over. I made this guy my god, and he wasn't worth anything!"

Audible sobs filled the room. While feeling weak at that moment from an emotional flashback, Kim's testimony about falling for the world's deceptions and experiencing the consequences provided a life lesson that a carefully crafted sermon could not do. Sister Dorinda, the leader of the Sister-2-Sister group walked up to Kim, squeezed her hand and whispered "thank you" to her.

It was then that Kim found her epiphany moment. That moment of breakthrough, recognizing with graphic detail the losses in her life, but ultimately coming back home, to Christ, to family, to values, and now, being in a place to share and impart these values to others.

Ladies, since we're talking about a fine piece of chocolate, let me drop you some "chocolate-isms," if you will so that, if you recognize the signs, you won't need damage control later. However, if you are already part of the army of the walking wounded, you can stanch the bleeding and move on.

The list of chocolate-isms a sista needs to know when she meets a guy.

1. If a guy asks you, "you think you're better than me?" you are, or else he would not ask you.
2. A package of cookies becomes a boring meal. Think of how tasty one jumbo cookie from the bakery tastes compared to a package of cookies from the supermarket, all the same flavor. Sistas, that cookie is your bargaining chip. If he opens the package too early in the relationship, it's simply another treat. Don't let him open the package so easily. He hasn't even paid for it.
3. Maintain the gold standard. A man knows quality when he sees it. If a sista is about educating her mind, building

her vocabulary, develop new skills, why settle for a guy who just has it all on the outside with Armani suits and Stacey Adams shoes. You settle for the rush that lasts for a minute, your gold standard drops. Think, gravitational pull. When a person stumbles down the steps, they don't just fall down one step and get up. They fall down the whole staircase.

## Discussion

The ways to move from relationship failure to relationship victory is formatted in question format since questions ultimately get a person to think, and thinking through critical choices and outcomes, sometimes with the help of a professional, can help the woman facing relationship failure get to the root of this failure, especially if there is a repeated pattern. When the root of that pattern is found and broken, the sista can shout, "hallelujah! I've got my victory.

1. Why is transparency important in healing? Imagine having an ill child who's sick, vomiting, and needs medical attention, but the mom admonishes the child to say, "I'm fine," when asked how they are doing. Eventually the child passes away when antibiotics could have helped. "How horrible!" any thinking person would say. Yet, isn't that what women in dysfunctional relationships do everyday? Many people were raised by the adage, "what goes on in this house stays in this house," and the healing and deliverance that could have taken place, had they went to the proper authorities,

never takes place, and sometimes the victim dies. If not physically, then perhaps emotionally, becoming a former shell of what they were. If you were locked in a car and couldn't breathe, if the window panes are clear, someone can see from the outside and get help. If those windows are tinted smoky black, nobody can see through. Transparency in a support group is a surefire way to grow as a group and to grow as individuals.

2.  What is your worth? In these tough economic times, more and more people are utilizing the services of financial planners. One of the questions are, "what is your net worth?" so, the client fills out the sheet with their assets on one side, their liabilities on the other, total each side, subtract, and find your net worth. If the total in liabilities is higher than the total in assets, then the net worth is negative. If the assets are higher, the net worth is positive. A woman has to know her assets and build them up. It takes work—lots of work for some of us, but in the end, it's worth it. What has more value? the fifty cent coin or the fifty dollar bill? You'll tear up the house looking for that bill come time to go grocery shopping. When you know your worth, ladies, you'll stop letting people imprint their vision on you. Now that's freedom!

3.  Why is the sista circle important? What if I just don't like to talk? Well, in my experience I have met people who have trust issues, and lack of trust is painful. From childhood, some people have learned that the significant people in their lives, (parents, particularly father figures) just cannot be trusted: they make a promise and break

it. While they are sometimes fun to be around, they only show up sporadically. If a young person is exposed to this type of disappointment and unreliability, it creates a wound of mistrust. Since experiences are imprinted upon a youngster, it's not surprising therefore that they pick men as partners that are unreliable, even when they're desperately trying to break out of this mold. Sista friends, if they are trustworthy, whole people, keep one another accountable. They'll speak the truth as they see it and insist on accountability. It's lonely to try to heal oneself, and by yourself, you may not have all the tools to make you whole. No man (or woman) is an island. No woman should stand alone.

4. Why are non negotiables important? Well, think of the proverbial spineless jellyfish that's shapeless, but wait! even they can sting. A non-negotiable that a woman absolutely will not tolerate protects her from further pain. If nothing an abuser does can make a victim angry enough to leave, eventually, the abuser, the playa, whatever you want to call him, gets bored. Some popular love songs by men, crooning for the love that's gone play into that theme. The lady got tired and she moved on. Now he realizes he had a good thing and can't get her back.

5. Are spiritual values really important? what if a person is a free thinker? (atheist) or non deity thinker? Everybody has some deity on some level, whether it is some lucky charm, talisman, saying, phrase or song that gets them through the day. Whatever it takes for them to make it. Studies have found that people with

a strong religious faith have lower blood pressure, less doctor visits, and shorter hospital stays. It's something to think about.

"The morality of compromise sounds contradictory. Compromise is usually a sign of weakness, or an admission of defeat. Strong men don't compromise it is said, and principles should never be compromised" Andrew Carnegie

Nina met Raul at a pre-Easter dinner at Crossroads Baptist Church. Coming from a traditional Episcopal background it was a different scene.
Living in a 3000 sq. ft. house on Overlook Drive, was a dream too big for Nina to think of.
"Raul was working full time as a computer tecchy. As he said, "these hands and this mind was made to compute. I know the parts of a computer, and what it needs, like I know my women".
And that was the beginning of Nina's downfall.
With all that Raul had going for him, Nina thought why is he so moody sometimes? Isn't this enough?
"Woman, you don't understand. Everything has a beginning and an ending. What you do with life is all in the middle in between."

Nina (to Raul) What is this? Answer me Raul! What is this!! Nina said, holding up an edition of Chocolate Guys and Gals magazine. Specifically, Chocolate Guys and Gals, for the 21st Century Discriminating Swinger. "Is this what that convention was about?? Answer me! Raul was briefly taken back by Nina's fit of rage, but then he regrouped. "Look woman, we're together, right? Stop being so doggone nosy! A man doesn't change overnight, and besides, you just don't understand.
Nina (with a whine in her voice), You're right! I don't understand. I keep the house the way you say you like it, and. Nina choked back the sobs as she saw Raul's facial expression change from sheepish to cruel.
A manipulator knows who to manipulate, and he has the tools at his disposal. There is a twisted dance that the manipulator does with his partner in order to keep her in line. When does the dance, so to speak, begin? Probably way back in childhood. Growing up, Nina was raised in a home where everybody was expected to do

as they were told; no discussions, you were expected to be seen and not heard.

(Nina's story) "I was the nice girl who finished last." There were two sisters and her cousin, who her parents helped to raise after her Aunt Marie died. They were always boisterous, once they would leave the Puritanical confines of the home. Nina, however, was always the quiet, deferential one. Nina, always loaning her books, school supplies, an occasional blouse or skirt (not that Cassandra, Alexis, or cousin Chelsea always asked before they borrowed).
"Oh, it's okay", Nina weakly smiled after Cassandra "the blouse thief" forgot to wash Nina's blouse after she borrowed it." Nina, the lender, but never the borrower, the middle child, the quiet one, whose presence was taken for granted, Who was Nina, really?
A girl must be taught her value, in order to become a woman, who knows her value, for if one does not know their value, others will put a price on them, and it just might be too low.

Raul, the successful technician who came up from the school of hard knocks. In Raul's words, "my dad, that punk, walked out on my mom and the four of us; my two sisters and my brother; we had to scrape by. My mom knew the deal leave before the first of the month, and find a new place, before the man comes knocking on the door, looking for the rent money. My mom always kept us together and would find another place to live. My mom, she's always been my first lady. She knew how to work off the books, collect that Mother's day check. Dress down, go to work, change, come back home, like she had nothing going on, so none of the nosey bodies could drop a dime on her. She's one smart lady.

Nina, in her words, was attracted to Raul from the moment she met him. Very savvy in a manner of speaking. She was very impressed with his self made image. In his words, "look to yourself first. The man upstairs helps those that help themselves." Nina worked as a representative for Mid-Atlantic gas and electric company, a position she was proud of. In her words, "I was never a social butterfly like my sisters and cousin, but I could hold a job down and people look to me for support and problem solving." When mid-Atlantic offered their employees a tuition discount program for an approved course of study, Nina jumped to it, and began her Master of Business Administration, and looked forward to moving up in the ranks of Mid-Atlantic. However Raul, persuasive demeanor, changed her plans.

(Raul, to Nina) "Look baby, you're a smart gal, or else I wouldn't have picked you to be my woman, and you wouldn't have picked me to be your man, right? I'll help take care of you until you find another job. After all, I'm a tech expert, it's a hot field. You trust me, don't you"? "Well, Raul, I was looking forward to this Master's you know? Will another company pay for (Raul, interrupting) Look, opportunity don't always come knocking. I'm moving up the ranks as well, and this house on Overlook Drive compliments us. Hey baby, you want this, don't you? (Nina, hesitating), "Uhm, I'm not really sure about this move and this job".

(Raul, raising his voice) What, you mean you don't trust me?? You act like I'm your parents, making you do what you don't really want to do. I'm your man! I'm your husband! I'm here giving you the good life! Think like a woman and not a little girl, baby!

Nina (quiver in her voice) "Okay, Raul, I just didn't want to rush into this. Of course I trust you, and I love you." With a sob, Nina grabbed and held Raul. "It's okay, baby, I shouldn't have come down so hard on you. I just need you to be in my corner and share my dreams with me.

(Fast forward; Nina and Raul bought the house on Overlook Drive and, adapting herself to her new environment, Nina convinced herself that this was her role to entertain and keep Raul and his friends happy. They enjoyed the tiny, hand made pizzas Nina created and, even though she wasn't a drinker, Nina learned how to tend bar like any professional. Still, she wistfully thought back of that opportunity at Mid-Atlantic. Raul's friends were a rather fast crowd but, Nina, the people pleaser, always tried to adapt.)

Somewhere in this relationship with Raul, Nina put her ambitions in the background. This educated, aspiring entrepreneur now was between jobs in a mini-mansion trying to please the friends of a self-absorbed husband. A teetotaler who now mixes drinks and smiles at the raunchy jokes of her husbands friends. Who is this Nina? Ladies, keep your identity. A the old saying goes, "show me your company and I'll tell you who you are."

*The compromise will always be more expensive than either of the suggestions it is compromising*
*Arthur Block*

Some appetites should never be awakened, and if awakened, they need to be killed. No matter how sophisticated postmodern society gets, some appetites are as primitive as the Mayan and

# A Fine Piece of Chocolate

Aztec cultures with their warrior gods whose appetites can only be appeased by human sacrifices. Raul's appetite extended above and beyond the loving arms of Nina, whose people pleasing only made her predictable, and well, boring. After the initial shock wore off of Nina about Raul's involvement with The Chocolate Swingers swap club, Raul's suggestions about doing this, "just once", began to wear down her no's.

(Nina thinking to herself) If Raul wants it this way, maybe I could swing better than all of them. After that, forget about it. Who else will know? (Fast forward) Nina became the living sacrifice, lying in the Templo Mayor, being fondled and penetrated every which way. *"I can't believe it!! (Screaming within herself. I am the living sacrifice!! No, I forgot! Jesus is! What am I doing here!!!)*

Afterwards, all the masked participants took off their masks, put them away, changed into their business attire and, without a word, took the elevators to the street level, where the parking attendant took them to their cars, and, went back to their world, again, without a word. Days and weeks went by, no discussion between Nina and Raul about this experience that fed his salacious appetite. But what affects the body affects the mind and the soul, and, the invisible strain between Nina and Raul became more and more apparent. What is left of a woman who participates in a wife swap? Nothing perhaps, but the remnants of a tattered soul, that, in Nina's case, becomes masked with more daiquiris, sleeping pills, and, a desire to escape for good.

No woman wakes up one day and decides to be in a wife swap to please her husband; not if she values herself. But some sisters don't recognize danger and that there is a time to walk away; even run. Ladies have to find their voice ad make it known, "oh no! not me; not that, ever. Find your voice and be heard. That is a lesson that Nina will have to learn.

Finally, the price of compromise, when is it ever too high?

How does one redeem one's self after violating every value that one has been brought up with? The flashbacks with Nina putting her hands over her ears and shutting her eyes, as if she could shut out the memories of her violation, and violation it was.

Unlike other violations, this one was agreed upon by the victim, and Nina was still a victim, nevertheless, without a covering for protection.

In ancient cultures during Hebraic times, a lamb was used as a covering for sin. The sacrificial lamb, in its innocence, is carried to the altar, throat slit, and the blood drained. The lamb is a most innocent, defenseless creature. It is killed to atone for the actions of the guilty. The lamb does not have defense mechanisms as other creatures have to protect itself from danger. It may not even have the sense to recognize danger and run. Curiosity can lead to compromise, as in, *maybe I can try this, just once. When one compromises, it creates an agony based upon how far away from one's principles does one deviate.* The scene at the Gentleman's Club was one where wine and spirits were flowing freely, perhaps to deaden the senses for what will eventually take place. The group was about 10 people, five male and five females. All the females were airbrushed and stylishly coiffed. Every one could have looked like a New York Sports Club success story. The doorbell rang, and it was the deliveryman for Mister Wright's Fine Wines and Spirits. Funny thing, Nina remembered that the liquor was many times more *plentiful than the food. The meal was light; guacamole dip, tortilla scoops and salsa, brought to each guest by cocktail waitresses in petite, party dresses. After all, better not to spoil the appetite for the coming attractions later.*

**Enter not into the path of the wicked, and go not into the way of evil men. Proverbs 4:14**. *Nina begins to stash bottles of wine to numb he pain she feels at compromising. It shows as she begins neglecting her appearance and her home. Things start looking untidy, and that is about the only thing that Raul is concerned about. Raul, still as ephemeral as ever, is coming and going on his own schedule, oblivious to the dire pain of his wife.*

*Although exhausted, Nina still can't sleep, and she begins to depend upon sleeping pills. Finally, the day comes when Nina decides to swallow the last 10 in the bottle: just end it all. There is a way which seems right unto a man, but the end thereof are the ways of death. Proverbs 14:12. "Jesus, forgive me", Nina thinks. "I don't know if ending it all is the way to go, but I know I was in Satan's domain the night of the club." She swallows the 4th pill. "I really didn't plan to leave this way, but it's time to make my grand exit." (She swallows 5, 6, &7.) Suddenly Nina gags, and feels her eyes bulging. Strange, these pills don't usually taste like anything. "Get it over with! Your journey is complete. There is nothing left." Nina looked around, not sure if the voice she heard was outside of her or within. Quickly, she*

*swallows 8, 9, and 10, and drifts off to a (hopefully) forever sleep to
a better place than where she is.*

*The tunnel is inky black; yet, Nina could make out the forms of bats
flying around and hears the sound of jeering laughter. "Oh no, what
is this???" a silent scream wells up in Nina's throat. "Is this a mistake
I really can't get out of?" maybe, FOREVER? She opens her mouth to
scream, but no sound comes out. Nina thinks to herself, "if I ever can
get out of this, I will never let anyone think for me again I swear!" At
that exact moment, a bright light, whiter than the brighteners her
grandmother used to whiten clothes, filled the atmosphere. The light
was so bright that even after Nina closed her eyes from brilliance,
her eyes still hurt. An instinctive fear and awe filled Nina's being,
and then she heard the Voice: "fear not; I know every thought and
plan that I have for you; plans to prosper you and not harm you; to
give you a future and a hope". Nina slowly opened her eyes as the
white brilliance muted somewhat. In the distance, she saw a figure of
a man in the distance, hands open, palm side up. There were black
holes going through the palms. Nina knew who she just encountered,
and she knew her life was not over yet; everything was going to be
alright.* "Weeping endures through the night, but joy comes in the
morning. Awe, dread, and appreciation just overwhelmed Nina,
and she convulsed with racking sobs that seemed to go on for the
next 100 years.

Nina felt her body being transported to another place, with bright
lights and beeping sounds. As she opened her eyes she sees, what?
masked figures standing over her. Is this a joke? "We almost thought
we lost you, said the kind voice of the doctor. Nina became aware
of the tubes in her arms and going down her nasal passages. She
started to speak, but then a contented peace enveloped her and
she drifted off to sleep.

Nina continued on her path to recovery, following a regimen of
appointments with her psychiatrist, social worker and dietician.
She looked forward to the twice weekly appointments with her
therapist, who coached her to help prepare to move on with her life
without Raul. "Some people are toxic", Georgia, the counselor said
in her opening statement to the group." "What is toxic?" Georgia
held up a bottle of a nondescript chemical, with a prominent skull
and crossbones on the front of the bottle. "How do you know when
a relationship is toxic?" Various answers went around the room
including: sad, angry, like I wanna fight, or, give up and go along
with it, Nina said softly. Several members turned around to look at

her. "when you really don't want to go along, right? Yeah, like, to things you really don't want to do.

Georgia encouraged Nina to email, call, or text her whenever she needed to talk, even between appointments. As Nina healed emotionally, her confidence grew. Her change in demeanor; no longer retreating into sadness alternating with biting sarcasm and rage at Raul, whenever he was home. Nina practiced trying out new hairstyles, and, when Raul was out with the family car, rather than sit around in the house, Nina simply took her keys, cash, and called a cab to take her into the city. Nina's quiet strength and confidence certainly wasn't lost on Raul, who sought to crush this independent streak emerging from his woman. Standing one's ground fosters personal growth. Woman! can't you do anything right! The mushrooms in these scrambled eggs looks like snail dung. At that moment, Nina stopped what she was doing and glowered at Raul for a full minute, without saying anything. Then she opened her mouth . . . .

You know, Raul, I've had plenty of time to think. Yeah, you came to me at a time when I was more like a girl than a woman, and showed me your side of life, and, for awhile there, I was in awe of you and tried to please you, like the way I spent my life always pleasing everyone else; keeping my mouth shut when I should have spoken, standing still when I should have walked away, going along with your sick ideas, and, (Raul, interrupting), "oh shut up woman, you're crazy_(Nina interrupting him, before he could finish the sentence, and beginning to raise her voice) "You know you're right! (laughing giddily), I was crazy, crazy about you and thinking you were worth something! You're just a piece of street trash dressed to look polished on top, rusty on the bottom. You know what, you're somebody I shouldda just got up and walked away from, with your trash talking self. You had nothing to offer me. I brought very thing into this relationship, I put the fine touches to this home, I gave up my career to follow you to this boondock while you talk your trash to whoever is dumb enough to listen. Furthermore, your accounts payable expenses exceeds your accounts receivable, meaning you're dead broke! Yeah, I've looked at the books Mr. CEO, CEO of what! I don't need you Raul, playing this charade! I'm not your slave anymore! I don't need you! I have a life, you polished on top, rusty on the bottom piece of garbage. I am redeemed, and I know the One who really loves me, and this is over! do you understand, OVER!!" Nina throws her coat on, purse and Bible in hand, and exits the house. Raul watches, slackjaw in astonishment, as she exits. How does respect work hand in hand with redemption? In Nina's case, she was able to value herself as she recognized her worth to her Creator, and then, she made her grand exit from the evil one.

Why is it that opposites attract? In the world of attraction, Why do nice gals fall for bad guys?

### Wifey or wife?

Saundra is 30ish, works as a bookkeeper for Samsung electronics. A self-described born again Christian, she actively serves in her church as an usher.

Alex is a self-described sports fanatic and "playa", whose specialty is professional women. He is especially attracted to "sexually reserved" women who believe a woman's rightful place is in the home and who seek to wait for the right man to "put a ring on it." To get a gal of that caliber is like getting 24kt. gold with platinum."

**Whatever value a woman puts on herself is what others will put on her.**

The name of the game may change, but it's still the same thing.

Alex pursues Saundra with cards and flowers. He meets her by chance in a pedestrian collision on the street. Let us continue from here.

Saundra is rushing to her job on East 56th st. and Park Avenue for the 8AM breakfast meeting. (to herself) "oh darn, that #6 train in the morning is always a killer." Out of breath, as she is attempting to beat the clock, at 7:56AM, she collides with a tall, brown skinned, handsome stranger, wearing a pinstripe suit jacket with dark, dress trousers. Dropping the packages in hand, Saundra became flustered "Let me help you", the stranger said as he bent to help Saundra pick up the packages. She felt a sense of irritation, not sure if it was at herself for not being more careful, or at him for not walking fast enough. At any rate, he helps her carry the packages, and pushes the heavy glass door with one hand, and hand the packages to her. "Thanks", she musters a quick smile and hurries to the breakfast meeting with the croissants.

Saundra represents many women of faith who are successful, professional, and perhaps the first in their family to go to college and graduate. She is well within the age range where many women are married with children, but many are not. It takes a certain amount of grace and fortitude to endure weddings and baby showers, and bridal showers for loved ones who teasingly remind you that you're not getting any younger, and, maybe you're even being "too picky", and think you're better than someone.

Saundra has a longing to get married, however, but just hasn't found the right one. She keeps a small stash of bridal magazines in the locked cabinet at her desk, and peruses through them from time to time, looking at the different color schemes of the different seasons. She likes burgundy and gold for the fall, and salmon pink and yellow for late spring and summer. She likes the color yellow, as, to her, it is a "happy and carefree color, and it goes well with so many other colors.

Midweek , Saundra gets a call from the front desk. Mary the mailroom clerk, gave Saundra a notice for her to go downstairs and sign for a package. For me? Saundra queried. "I didn't order anything. Now, Mary was someone who sometimes like to play practical jokes, and Saundra was in no mood for fun and games. A package for you, no kidding, Mary insisted. Saundra took the elevator from the 17th floor to the main level, and walked over to front desk security. Melvin, the short, serious faced security agent had a large bouquet of flowers on the desk, pen in hand, waiting for her to sign. It was a rather large, beautiful bouquet of yellow roses, navy blue zinnias, adorned with baby's breath." For me! "Saundra shouted, forgetting the atmosphere of the building. "Who sent them?" she shouted again. Melvin just shrugged and said, "name's on the card". Saundra quickly signed, and bolted away with this package, nearly tripping in her Easy Spirit sling back heels. Saundra caught the express elevator to the 17th floor, and, holding them down by her side so as not to be too conspicuous, carries them back to her desk and finds the card, simply signed, "Alex, 51st and 3rd. For a second she wondered (her mind drew a blank. Then, she remembered the tall, caramel complexioned young man that she ran into, earlier that week. She vaguely remembered them exchanging names. She certainly did not remember exchanging last names. There was a 718 telephone number underneath Alex's name. With beating heart, Saundra takes out her cellphone and program Alex's telephone number into her contact list.

**What you imagine becomes your reality**
Her mind wonders: where does he work? These flowers are her favorite colors. They'd be perfect for a spring wed—(wait a minute, you're jumping too fast!) that was her superego speaking. There

are men who draw women to them like magnets, because they seem to have the ability to read them. Saundra has a deep desire to "stop looking for and finding the wrong men, and just to be held by the right one." (superego to Saundra, as she takes out the March 2000 issue of Bride's magazine, the color scheme of those purple and gold zinnias), "now you're moving too fast! You don't know if he's married or seeing other women. Does he have a good job or is he simply a hustler!" Saundra closed the magazine before her superego could continue and spoil her fantasy.

At the end of the workday, Saundra closes off the lights in her cubicle, files away the documents in their appropriate folders, and boards the express elevator to the first floor. She cradles the bouquet of flowers in her left arm, and the leather burgundy purse in her right hand, holding her Metrocard. Thoughts of, "should I or shouldn't I call him, played like a ping pong game inside of her head, as she stood on the crowded platform, awaiting the #6 train. In the pit of her gut, she knew what she was going to do.

Later on, as she got home to her apartment in the Parkchester Gardens complex, Saundra dialed Alex's phone number, but only got his recorded message. Trying to make her voice sound as light hearted and nonchalant as possible, she called back again, 3 hours later. "Hi Alex! Gee, that was a nice surprise. The flowers are lovely. You have a good night." Click. Ten minutes later, Saundra's cellphone rings. She wonders if Alex was available and just chose to screen his calls and not answer.

"Hello?" Who's calling?" (brief silence and then a mid-bass voice responds, "Alex, to whom your wish is my command, my dear.") Saundra broke out in a fit of laughter which she could not control. The more she tried to control it, the more she just continued to laugh.
Alex (thinking to himself) "I know just what she likes."
Saundra recovered, both exhilirated and terribly embarrassed by her uncontrolled emotions, not knowing that this was the beginning of uncontrolled emotions.
**Control your emotions, or they will control you.**

Their conversation lasted a little under an hour; peak minutes, Saundra ruefully noticed, as it was before 9PM, weekday.
"How did you get my full name and department? Saundra queried.
"Let's just call that Alex the investigator's secret", Alex said.

"Oh, but I'd like to really know. After all, you don't need to know everything about me." Saundra then felt uncomfortable about what sounded like an awkward sounding statement.

"Is there something I shouldn't know? Maybe I just might like it," Alex said. Saundra flushed at the mildly sexually explicit connotation of Alex's words. "Whaddya up to this Saturday?" Alex asked. Saundra attempted to sound nonchalant by saying, "I have to look at my calendar. Sometimes I have to work weekends."

"Very well then. I'll call back Thursday evening."

Thursday came, Alex called, Saundra confirmed.

**Decisions build your destiny**

Saundra continued to see Alex. They really never discussed matters of faith. Many times, in their conversations, they would laugh and go back to that chance meeting on 56th and Park Avenue. Nagging doubts plagued Saundra about the faith issue, since she was devout about her faith and bringing friends and family to the Lord. Every Sunday, as Saundra performed her ushering duties, escorting the visitors and members to their seats, she would wistfully think of Alex when she would watch the various married couples take their seats as a family. This Sunday as usual, something was said from the pulpit that would bring Saundra to conviction, once again.

"And today, we're going to have one of those announcements", Pastor Theodore Brown announced with a smile, from the pulpit. Audible murmurs went around the auditorium and women, moreso that men, looked around, and began giggling. After a lengthy pause that seemed like forever, but in reality was only 45 seconds, Pastor Brown continued. I am pleased to announce the engagement of, "Brother Anthony James Smith to Sister Cynthia L. Goodwill." Saundra jerked herself to complete attention. Cynthia??? Old fashioned, schoolmarm looking Cynthia! And 50 something at that!

Cynthia taught various classes in the Sunday School division and made her standards clear: no man with young children. That means baby mama drama, and, no divorced men. Unless his wife is dead, he's still a married man. Jesus said, "whoever marries a divorced woman causes her to commit adultery, and, I didn't come this far for my Lord to say, "depart from me, you adulterer." These discussions came up from time to time when Cynthia would teach the single adult class. The young adults tried to convince Cynthia that times have changed, but, Cynthia stood her ground firmly.

Pastor Brown continued: "Here is an example of a couple who take their walk with Christ seriously. Brother Anthony is active in the men's ministry and ministers at the men's House of Detention every third Sunday. When we talked in the study, he said, "Pastor, I said I'd never marry again after my wife died, but the Lord put Cynthia on my heart, and, here I am today, asking you to bless this commitment."

And ladies, you see, God works in his timing. There is a season for every purpose Anthony and Cynthia found each other in the work of the Lord, and let the Lord mold and shape their destiny. Ladies and gentlemen, I'm saying this more for the ladies, "don't get unequally yoked! Don't let anyone tell you the Word isn't for these times. IT Is! The world's values are not God's values. Period!

Each word of Pastor Brown hit Saundra like a sledgehammer right in her heart. "Oh no, stop, please! (Saundra felt her eyes fill with tears and she had to look down for a minute and discretely dab her eyes with the tissue in her white gloved hand.

So, why was Saundra so sad at the announcement of a fellow sister's engagement? Well, for on thing, Saundra began seeing Alex before she got any signals from him about his faith walk. On occasion, Saundra attempted to discuss activities in the church, or something Pastor Brown said, Alec would change the subject or continue talking about whatever he was talking about. *For what fellowship hath light with darkness" II Corinthians 6:14*

Darkness can masquerade as light, but only for so long.

*Saundra's story continues.*

Saundra passed the potroast and julienne carrots towards Alex at the neatly set dining room table in her home.

Alex (to Saundra) "What's wrong with my sweetie?

Saundra "oh nothin".

Alex: come on. I know when something's wrong with my baby.

Saundra: "just conflicts, I guess."

Alex: *(shrinking back from touching her cheek:)* "Is it that pastor again? You know, baby, you can't let things get to you. I know about the church and the things they say, how they brainwash people."

Saundra: "but, I know what my convictions are and Alex, (pause, sometimes the things we do leads to sin, and, (voice trails off) "I don't feel so good (*Saundra wondered how a chance encounter on 51st & Park Avenue six months ago could have led to so many close encounters again and again.)*

Cynthia and Saundra are two different women with the same challenges; well into their adult years, both have a desire to get married, serving in their church, but two different outcomes;

they both built upon their decisions differently and had different outcomes.

## Conflicts lead to crossroads

When two people with different objectives come together, there is only one result: conflict.

Saundra attempted to call Alex a third time, and nearly swore under her breath, but she caught herself. Alex agreed to go with her to see the Messiah concert, and now it was two hours before the concert and she still hadn't heard from him. *"Good thing I have the tickets with me", Saundra thought, "or this would cost me $70 + a handling fee.*

Saundra checked her watch again, hoping against hope that it was not time to leave yet, and Alex would have at least called. "Oh oh! I better leave now or I'll be late, Saundra thought. The tension in her jaw and in her heart was becoming more and more frequent these days.

This was the second time in as many weeks that Alex was either late or just plain missing in action. Saundra covered up the all too familiar pain in her heart, the familiarity of relationships gone sour. It was difficult for Saundra to focus on the beauty of the orchestral accompaniments of her favorite classical musical, without Alex there.

In the middle of the second act, a breathless Alex came in, apologizing, saying, "scuse me, scuse me, as he passed through the rows, being careful not to step on anyone's shoes in the dark.

"Okay, so, maybe he isn't too unreliable, Saundra thought.

"Baby, I'm so sorry I'm late, Alex murmured in her ear, as he squeezed her right hand.)

Saundra noticed that he kept his coat and scarf on. When she questioned him about it, he just said, "I'm okay babe. Let's just watch this." She also noticed that he checked his watch several times.

Although her eyes were fixed on the musicians and she unconsciously nodded along with the arrangements, Saundra's mind was completely elsewhere.

"Oh well so much for $70 tickets and a conversation about faith," she thought to herself. As Saundra and Alex left Lincoln Center, the tension between them was thick enough to cut with a knife. A surge of anger kept welling up within Saundra that she kept swallowing down like bile. Finally, the volcanic eruption just came out.

# A Fine Piece of Chocolate

"Alex!, if there is something you need to tell me, just say it and let's be done with it, OK? I really don't like game playing, OK?"

Alex knew the routine. When Saundra's voice took on a certain tone and she kept saying, "OK", everything was not okay, and it usually meant an encounter of the loud kind. Usually, their arguments were in Saundra's apartment, where they hung out most of the time. This would be the first outburst in public, and Alex was not one to endure public displays of hostility.

"Look baby," he said, his voice equally tense, "I'm sorry, OK, I had to take care ah some business."
"What business! Saundra demanded.
"My business!" and don't talk to me like that out here, woman," Alex hissed at her, ignoring the stares of passers by.
"You know, you got that lying spirit within you and you keep messing with my feelings, my time, and my life! and THAT'S NOT OK, ALEX GRANT!!
Alex (noticing the pedestrians slowing down to watch a possible free show while keeping a safe distance.
"Woman, you keep your voice down, you hear? I don't talk my business in the street. We'll discuss it when we get home, and that's it!
In hysteria, Saundra grabbed Alex's top button of his coat. He looked surprised and pushed her away roughly, so much so, she almost lost her balance. Saundra felt a fleeting sense of surprise at Alex's lack of warmth toward her. Realizing she had a choice to make right then she shouted "You no good punk! Just go! Leave me alone! You're just fake!

Saundra took off like a bullet and ran towards 66th street, catching the downtown local to Times Square to transfer to the shuttle going to the East side. This was enough time for her to sob and get the first part of her emotions out of her system.
Righteous women need to hold to their values, no matter how convincing the circumstances may seem. Saundra very much desired to attain the status of wife, and to a godly, caring husband. Unfortunately, she was taken in and seduced by Alex's charm and charisma. Alex came to Saundra as a thoughtful gent, who would pick up her packages when they fell, surprise her with flowers; his attentiveness and street smarts led her down a familiar path of temporary satisfaction, heartache and despair. When Saundra saw that Alex was not the man that she hoped for, she became

disillusioned, and lost respect for him and resented him. The final slap of humiliation came when Saundra found herself going through envelopes and shirts that Alex left at her home. She came across a note addressed to "Rose." "Hi, my little wifey, everything was good. You know, save the last dance 4 me.

Wifey?? Who is this Rose woman? Saundra's mind was racing at a thousand megabytes a minute. So many questions; was she a plaything Alex kept on the side? Did she know that Alex was already committed to her, and they were discussing their future together? After all, Alex and Saundra saw each other most days after work and he was working hard in that jewelry appraisal business. Who was Rose, anyway? Saundra looked for evidence and then, finding none, she shredded Alex's shirts that he left in her closet.

## Wifey or wife?

Saundra went through the motions of a courtship, had promises, but no real substance behind it. Alex wooed Saundra with attention; lots of compliments about everything she did; her cooking, her talent for decorating her home tastefully, and even her faith. As a matter of fact, Alex oftentimes complimented her on her devout faith, and told her she is, "just the woman he is looking for to be the mother of his children. Although Alex confessed to being a "lapsed Catholic", he would often quote the Sermon on the Mount, where Jesus would proclaim, "Blessed are the poor in spirit, for theirs is the kingdom of heaven." Alex would comfort and encourage Saundra during the times when she would fret about not having enough money to pay for all of her expenses at the end of the month. Alex told Saundra she is perfect "wife material", and indeed, the relationship took on the qualities of husband wife in every way but name only. She felt like his wife, and, for a season, it sure felt good.

*"Flee fornication. Every sin that a man doeth is without the body, but he that comitteth fornication sinneth against his own body. (I Corinthians 6:18)*

**Relationship failure leads to repentance and restoration**

Saundra (to head of the usher board) "I have to take time off to take care of some personal things," Saundra explained to Sister Mack, as she handed her her resignation. Saundra, anything I can help you with? Sister Mack looked both concerned and alarmed." "Uh no. Me and the Lord have to work out a few things. I'll be back soon. I promise."

Saundra fled the room before a wave of tears engulfed her. As soon as she left the building and was sure she was out of earshot of anybody, she let out a tremendous wail. Racking sobs shook her frame. Looking upward towards the sky she cried out, "Oh God! I failed you again! Again and again I failed you! How come I can't get it right once and for all, Lord?"

Why is it that we are sometimes attracted so strongly to people or things that are not good for us? Think of the moth attracted to the flame.

**Redemption leads to recovery**

*What becomes of the broken hearted, who that love has now departed. I know I got to find, some kind of peace of mind, baby (taken from, What Becomes of the Broken Hearted, by David Ruffin)*

The David Ruffin tune played in Saundra's headphones as she ran the treadmill in the Lucille Roberts gym. It seemed that WBLS was playing a lot of classic R&B that reflected Saundra's state of mind. Yet the songs were therapeutic in their own way. Saundra threw herself into her job as well as her exercise routine. Having David's cookies and a coffee after work every day was starting to tell on her waistline.

Later on, at home, the telephone rings. Saundra picks up. Pam, a sister friend who attended the winter women's winter retreat was on the other end.

"Hey girl, how's it going?" "Oh great!" Saundra replied with an enthusiasm that she really did not feel. Pam spoke at length about the challenges she had as a physical therapist in North Central Bronx hospital, and Saundra gave the appropriate "um-hms" during the conversation. Saundra was getting ready to change the subject when Pam invited her to a Women's conference on healing and restoration from relationships.

"Ah, Pam, let me get back you on that one, OK? I was just about to start dinner and—Pam interrupted to start a new conversation on how the Lord healed her after she loaned her last boyfriend $1,000 to fix his car and he didn't pay her back, and she really wanted to kill him, and—"more drama," Saundra thought to herself. Finally she cut in during an appropriate pause and said, "Ah , Pam listen, I really got to go now and hey, it was great talking to you. I may see you there."

Pam: "Great! Let me give you the date, time, and address."

Saundra took down the information out of politeness, although she really didn't intend to go. Lately, Saundra began experiencing what can only be described as a "Blank" feeling inside her, whenever she was around the sisters and brothers in Christ, sharing their faith at the Tuesday testimonial services. She didn't feel the enthusiasm that she heard others express at the meetings. Saundra wondered whether or not she was losing her faith.

The following Friday evening, Saundra looked forward to breaking bread with her colleagues from the sales department at an early dinner meeting. "Perhaps", she reasoned to herself, "I can advance my career attending after work meetings. The church meetings on Friday could get lengthy. As she checked her email, Saundra noticed with dismay that the early dinner meeting was cancelled. "What?? I was looking forward to this! I mean, I got dressed up for this and now have nowhere to go. Then came the thought, Redemption and Restoration.
Reluctantly, Saundra dialed Pam's cellphone number to confirm that she would be joining Pam at the meeting after all. Saundra pulled the phone away as Pam yelled, "oh great! Praise the Lord! You will love this woman of God!"

Saundra was surprised, as she walked into the conference room, to see this diminutive woman of Jewish lineage, addressing a mainly African-American group. The meeting was already in progress, and Dr. Lowe was describing her background. "I came out of Kabbala, and I didn't really learn about love and acceptance. I went from one relationship to another, and it was not until I came to the end of myself that I realized that I didn't have all the answers. I didn't even know the right questions." That last statement caught Saundra's attention. Not asking the right questions, not considering a man's motives. One by one, the ladies, sitting around the large conference room table, described relationship challenges with parents, boyfriends, husbands, sexual abuse, financial abuse. As the stories abounded, Saundra began feeling a sense of camaraderie with these women, most of whom she just met for the first time. Everyone experienced the loss of a significant other in their lives.
Then came time for intercessory prayer with the crisis counselors who themselves were delivered from the cycle of abuse. Nervously, Saundra made her way towards the front of the room and the counselor held both of Saundra's hands warmly and smiled. "And, what is your need tonight, Sister?"

Saundra, who took pride in keeping her emotions under wraps, burst into tears. "I stopped seeing this guy two months ago. I luh-loved him," as she pronounced the word, "love", she emitted a howl that sounded like another world. One part of her wanted to keep it in, another part wanted to let it go. "I don't like falling apart in front of this stranger and this group of women," Saundra thought. Frantic thoughts of loss of control filled her being. Although other women were going through prayer and deliverance, Saundra felt like the only woman there. "Oh please, jee—she pleaded with God mentally, "make the pain go away." Wave after wave of emotions engulfed her until finally Saundra collapsed on the floor from exhaustion.

When she came to, she felt confused and thought it was the next day, but it was just one half hour later. Two of the ladies helped her to her feet. "That was the Holy Spirit's job, not mine," Dr. Lowe said to her. Dr. Lowe gazed at Saundra steadily and said firmly, "young lady, walk in your deliverance and realize you are free."

From that moment on, Saundra was peaceful, more peaceful that in the past when she thought she had peace. As soon as she felt the timing was right, she contacted Sister Mack and asked if she could be reinstated to the usher board.

"Of course, Saundra", Sis. Mack replied. No one could fill that post as well as you could.

Saundra carried out her ministry duties with a newfound zeal that she never had before. "who's the new beau, honey" nosey Sister Pierce asked. That glide in your stride and pep in your step must be a new man."

"The man is the carpenter from Galilee," Saundra smiled.

As the months went by, Saundra's thoughts of Alex were so vague, he didn't cross her mind anymore. She took his picture out of the frame and ripped it up. Then, she thought again, and tossed both the frame and the picture in the garbage. The jewelry pieces she tossed out as well. The clothes, she donated to charity. Time to clear out the old and get ready for the new. This is a new season.

During the revival service for the southern New York district, Saundra had the opportunity to usher a certain young man to his seat every night. He always sat on the side of the assembly where she was posted. He was a minister in training at Franklin Avenue Baptist Church in Brooklyn. Brother Thomas Stewart Sawyer was his name. Quiet, and rather reserved, he possessed a quiet strength that Saundra found intriguing. Thomas exchanged his phone numbers with Saundra, and over the days, weeks and months he would call her and they would talk about the scriptures, and his engineering studies at Brooklyn College. After about eight weeks of telephone conversation, Brother Thomas asked Saundra to have dinner with him at BBBG's. Although traveling from Brooklyn to Parkchester, he was always on time. He brought a bouquet of carnations and red roses on their first date. While not as colorful as Alex, Thomas had a sincerity that was apparent to all who met him. Like a leaf that starts out as a bud and unfolds slowly, Thomas and Saundra's friendship developed. He may not have had her heart thumping, but she could trust him and she truly enjoyed his company.

After about 8 months of dating, phone calls, and a quick kiss on the cheek at the door, Thomas called her and told her one day that he had a job opportunity with a company and he didn't want to forfeit his scholarship. Anyway, the message sounded rather confusing, and Saundra felt dread starting to creep up on her. "I wonder what this is?" she thought. Well, if it's over, I'm glad I didn't let myself get too serious about him. That evening, Thomas was running behind schedule, usually he was always on time. A lump of fear rose in Saundra's throat as memories of Alex's latenesses and disappearances came flooding back. Then, the doorbell rang. A serious faced Thomas was at the door. "Saundra, sit down, Thomas said gravely as he led her to the couch. He licked his lips nervously. "I went to the Lord about some things I needed to talk to Him about, and, one thing I said was, "Lord, I need a wife, but not just any woman could be my wife. I know you've been through some rough things, but I want you to know I would never hurt you in any way. I'm sorry I'm late, but I was asking the Lord to help prepare you and me for this. Slowly, Thomas reached into his inner jacket pocket and pulled out a small black, velvet box. Saundra's eyes grew wide as saucers. She put both hands to her mouth. "Oh no . . . Thomas continued and took her left hand, which was shaking wildly. "Saundra, will . . . you . . . marry me?

"Oh (sobbing) yes! yes! She threw her arms around him and the two of them held each other tighter than they ever did. He kissed her gently on her cheeks, lips and forehead. "I love you Saundra. Saundra was sobbing too loudly to say anything.
*(Jeremiah 29:11 "For I know the thoughts that I have towards you, saith the Lord, thoughts to prosper and not harm you, to give you a future and a hope.)*
The courtship flowed beautifully, like a calm ocean. Thomas, like a gentleman, would take Saundra home and not linger at the

home too long. "I just don't want to open any doors to temptation," Thomas explained.

Finally, it was Saundra's turn for "one of those special announcements." The thunderous applause and standing ovation at Pastor Brown's announcement made Saundra realize she was in the right place, at The right time, and experiencing love for all the right reasons."

Six months later, standing before Pastor Brown and the company of well wishers that Saturday in July, as Saundra gazed into the deep brown eyes of her loving husband, as Pastor Brown pronounced them husband and wife, Saundra knew that there was a clear difference between a wifey and a wife.

# Chocolateisms

What is a cholateism? Author Jacqueline R Banks defines a chocolateism as a nugget of wisdom that a woman obtains from life experience in dealing with a man, particularly a fine piece of chocolate. Below is a list of situations that many women will find themselves in. Knowing how to think and respond is vitally important.

<u>Look before you leap.</u>

- If, in the middle of a disagreement a man asks, "do you think you're better than me?" Chances are you are! See, a man recognizes quality and a gold standard when he sees it. A woman who is about educating her mind, keeping physically fit, developing new skills, ends up settling for a guy who just gives her a rush and dresses well. Please! There's more to life than Stacey Adam shoes and Armani suits. Chances are he's still paying it off on his credit card.

- If his standards are lower than yours in one way, your standards will drop in all ways. Why? You ask. It's because there's a pulling downward. It's a gravitational pull. When a person stumbles down the steps, they don't just fall down on one step and get up. They fall down the whole flight usually.

- Beware of junk food love. The substandard man is like a junk food diet. A junk food diet is inferior to organic. If he criticizes your standards and choices you need to say, "I have standards. They're mine, and I don't bend them or break them for anybody.

*Amos 3:3—two cannot walk together except they be agreed.*

## Know Your Achilles Heel when it comes to toxic men

- Every woman has an Achilles Heel or weakness when it comes to a certain type of man. Look back into your past to find your Achilles Heel. You like those hot young things that end up having you feel like an old cougar leave them alone! You're not going to be 20 again.

  Or the take charge dude who's really a control freak. Come on! Do you really need someone to tell you what clothes to put on every day and how to fix your hair? I thought that's why you left your mama's house in the first place.

- Don't miss your calling fixing a substandard man.
  Life is too short. You go your way and I'll go mine.
  I wish you the best.

## THE END

# Ten Secrets to Move From Relationship Failure to Relationship Victory

1. Have a sister circle of friends and family that are affirmative towards you. You are meant to live in community with others.
2. Share <u>A Fine Piece of Chocolate</u> with struggling women.
3. Recognize that you do have an inner voice and listen to it. That hesitation may be holding you back from disaster.
4. Maintain a strong devotional and prayer life. It's a battle out there for your soul.
5. Be willing to listen to and respond affirmatively to the concerns of those around you who have your best interest. They might discern something that you don't yet recognize.
6. Read the Bible, especially the Proverbs.

7. Have an accountability partner that you can share your struggles. Make sure they are a person with integrity who will not broadcast your business.
8. Have non-negotiables you will not compromise, ever.
9. Have a hobby.
10. Believe in yourself.

# Acknowledgements

This work would not be possible if it were not for the following people in my life:

My parents, Russell and Gwen Banks who inculcated me with the values that carry me to this day.

My Brother, Deacon Stephen Banks, a righteous piece of chocolate who has the sensitivities that men need in this day and age.

My wonderful son Trevor, who quietly encouraged me and believed I would complete this monumental project;

Deacon Calvin Hawkins, my spiritual big brother,

A host of extended family and friends, who were supporters of me in letting me know they have my back: SWARM ministry, headed by sister Georgette Turner; an awesome leader if there ever was one! Bishop Carlton T. Brown and First Lady Lorna Brown, a living example of a successful marriage, sister friends Pam, Pat, Joan, Liz, Dr.

Lillian Glass, author of Toxic Men, whose studies of men helped to sharpen my knowledge so I can help others, and ultimately, the guidance of the Triune Godhead, which has carried me for all my adult life.